Love is
a time of enchantment:
in it all days are fair and all fields
green. Youth is blest by it,
old age made benign:
the eyes of love see
roses blooming in December,
and sunshine through rain. Verily
is the time of true-love
a time of enchantment — and
Oh! how eager is woman
to be bewitched!

POOR MARY

The Herron family was threatened by divorce. Mary found it impossible to believe her husband's 'story', whilst Garth, hurt and angry, walked out of the house. Neither really wanted a divorce — Mary wanted the truth and Garth wanted her trust. What Mary needed was a change of scene to put things into perspective — she had to travel six thousand miles before she succeeded, and another six thousand before she found happiness.

Books by Clare Breton Smith
in the Ulverscroft Large Print Series:

THE AWAKENED HEART

CLARE BRETON SMITH

◆

POOR MARY

Complete and Unabridged

ULVERSCROFT
Leicester

First published in Great Britain in 1969

First Large Print Edition
published October 1992

British Library CIP Data

Smith, Clare Breton
  Poor Mary.—Large print ed.—
Ulverscroft large print series: romance
I. Title
823.914 [F]

ISBN 0–7089–2737–8

Published by
F. A. Thorpe (Publishing) Ltd.
Anstey, Leicestershire
Set by Words & Graphics Ltd.
Anstey, Leicestershire
Printed and bound in Great Britain by
T. J. Press (Padstow) Ltd., Padstow, Cornwall

Part One

Mary

MARY was asleep when Mrs. White opened the bedroom door, deftly balancing the breakfast tray in her hand.

"Good morning, Mrs. Herron. Real nice day it is, too," she said quietly but nevertheless heartily.

Stirring, Mary half-opened her eyes, yawned. Automatically she looked at the second bed. It was empty. Of course! Neatly covered with the green bedspread. She looked away from it quickly and at the plump, grey-haired woman bringing the tray to the bed.

"Thanks, Mrs. White."

There was orange juice, kidneys and bacon, toast, marmalade, butter and coffee. Mrs. White believed in plenty of food.

Mrs. White was moving round the room, drawing back the curtains to let in the sunshine, and talking.

"Ever so quiet the house is, Mrs. Herron.

3

Sort of unnatural-like, isn't it. It doesn't seem like a home any more. Everything's so neat and tidy. No tobacco about, no damp towels on the bathroom floor. And now the children've gone, too. There just isn't anything for me to do, Mrs. Herron."

Mary ate slowly, though had she been asked what she was eating, she wouldn't have known. Now Mrs. White was standing at the foot of the bed, her arms folded, her uneven teeth, with several gaps, exposed in a nervous smile, her face embarrassed.

"I was wondering. Mrs. Herron, if you could manage without me for a week or so. I mean, there isn't much to do with Mr. Herron away and the children back at school, and I'm real worried about my old man . . . "

"Your old man? Oh, yes, of course, your husband," Mary said, suddenly remembering that Mr. White had been rushed to hospital a few days before. "How is he . . . by the way?"

"Not too well by any means, Mrs. Herron. They're sending him to London, to the Heart Hospital there. I've a cousin what has a flat in Bayswater and she said I could stay with her. I'd be ever so much obliged if you could spare me. You see, I feel I ought to visit him every day like. It's a long day in hospital without visitors, isn't it . . . "

Mary Herron stifled a sigh. Mr. White might be ill but Mary knew very well that was not why Mrs. White wanted a 'few weeks off'. She would have heard the rumours, the gossip that was going around.

It followed Mary wherever she went. She knew what they were saying.

'Poor Mary . . . '

'Who'd have thought it! Such a happy couple. Twenty years of happiness and now . . . '

'And those sweet children. Poor Mary . . . '

No one had said anything but she could read it in their eyes. There was a sudden silence when she entered a room. She knew they'd been talking about her. She could almost hear the hissing whispers. 'Poor Mary . . . Poor Mary.'

Mrs. White was probably looking for

a more permanent job. No doubt she thought that if the marriage was breaking up, then they'd sell the house.

Sell the house?

Nearly choking, Mary coughed and spluttered. Finally the warm coffee soothed her throat.

"Of course that's all right, Mrs. White," Mary said, pushing the tray to one side, running her hand through her long, loose brown hair. "I'll miss you . . . "

Mrs. White beamed and swooped down on to the tray, lifting it triumphantly. "Oh, no you won't, Mrs. Herron. There just isn't anything to do with you on your own. Look, is it all right if I work fast and go off this morning? I mean, I've a lot to arrange and . . . "

"Quite all right . . . " Mary pushed back the bedclothes, swung her feet out of bed, fumbling for her slippers.

At the doorway, Mrs. White paused, her lined, reddish face unhappy. "I was wondering, Mrs. Herron . . . I mean, Mr. Herron usually pays me about now . . . "

Mary stiffened. "Of course. Your wages . . . " She looked round the

6

room wildly. She hadn't a clue how much Garth paid the woman for her services.

"I . . . I . . . "

It was the same with everything, she thought angrily. Garth had paid all the bills, and had now walked off, leaving her to cope.

And then she remembered. She slipped on her dark green dressing-gown and crossed the room to the small walnut escritoire he had given her for a birthday present ten years before. She pulled open one of the drawers and there was a neat little pile of envelopes, each with a name typed on it.

She'd forgotten all about them. Now she remembered that when Garth had come back to see the children, choosing a time when he knew she would be out, he had told Voi to tell her mother that he'd left cheques for the bills to be paid.

Her fingers shuffled through the envelopes. She found the right one and turned. "Mrs. White. Here you are . . . "

Mrs. White beamed. "There! Isn't that just like Mr. Herron? Such a thoughtful man. He thinks of everything . . . "

Except of me, Mary thought bitterly as she handed over the envelope and Mrs. White's portly but amazingly-brisk-moving form vanished and the door shut.

Mary stood for a moment, her hands pressed to her face. How could Garth have done this to her? she asked herself for the hundredth time. Twenty years of happiness and then, he could do a thing like this to her.

She bathed leisurely for there was nothing for her to do that morning. No committee meetings. No shopping. When she returned to the bedroom, the bed was made, the furniture polished, the windows wide open, letting in the fresh nip of September air.

Mary went to the wardrobe and chose a blue shirt-waister frock. It was rather faded but clean. She took out a white cardigan for, in the shade, the wind could be cool. She thrust her feet into sandals, brushed her hair, twisted it in a coil, fastening it with hairpins. She leaned forward to brush her nose with powder, then outline her mouth, and then turned away. Once you reach thirty-nine years, you stop worrying about your looks, if you've any sense, she always told herself.

Going to the window where the long white net curtains were fluttering, Mary remembered how Garth had disliked net curtains.

"It isn't as if anyone can see you," he'd said. "After all, there's nothing between us and the sea."

"I've always had net curtains," she had explained. "I'd feel sort of . . . well, naked without them."

Garth had understood. He always had understood. At least, in those days.

Now she leant against the wall, pleating the net in her fingers, as she looked down at the wide expanse of garden, then at the road, and the long stretch of marsh going down to the distant line of silver where the sea sparkled in the sunshine.

The garden was pretty. In a conventional way, she thought, a little startled by her own thoughts, for she had never thought that before! Neat rows of roses, still in flower, a wide border of dahlias. A circular bed of red chrysanthemums.

Everything neat and tidy and completely without character.

She half-closed her eyes. She could remember a time when she and Garth had spent most weekends in the garden. Then, when Voi was on the way, her mother had advised her to go slow, so she had given up gardening, and somehow Garth had lost interest, too. Now he paid a local nursery gardener to attend to the garden.

Turning slightly round, resting her head against the wall, she thought how odd, now she came to think of it, that there were so many things they had once shared and now neither of them were interested in. Golf! They had played a lot in the early days but she had got tired easily after Robbie's birth, and had stopped. And then Garth had stopped playing, too.

They had been so happy together in those early days. Not only playing golf and gardening but talking. Then something must have happened and everything was different. There was nothing more discouraging, Mary thought, than trying to talk to a newspaper, behind which your husband retreated.

In those early days, Garth was always there to turn to in times of trouble. But now . . . !

Mary's fingers played with the net, twisting it into strange shapes as she stood there, chilled by the September sea breeze, yet unable to move as her thoughts took control.

The sun had been shining, too, that day it had all begun. She had driven her Mini car into Bexhill to do some shopping and had given old Mrs. Jenkins a lift. Mary hardly knew her, only seeing her at church or at one of the church socials Mary dutifully attended. Driving to Bexhill, Mary listened vaguely to the endless story of Mrs. Jenkins' wonderful son, but near the town Mrs. Jenkins asked her to drop her off at the station.

"Visiting your son?"

"Oh, no. He's in New Zealand. Married and got three children. No, I'm visiting my sister in Battle. Not too well."

After Mrs. Jenkins had gone into the station, Mary, having helped her out of the car, saw the Jag. The same model as

11

theirs. Then she recognised the number. It *was* their Jag!

Puzzled, she strolled over to where the Jag was parked. She recognised Garth's umbrella on the back seat. The doors were locked. Of course, for Garth was careful.

But what was it doing in Bexhill? she wondered. Garth always drove to Cooden station, parking the Jag there until he came back from London in the evening.

The question puzzled her. It seemed to haunt her. It was so unlike Garth. Why, ever since they were married, twenty years before, and had come to live at Mon Repos, Garth had commuted to London by train from Cooden. Twenty years, from Cooden. So what was his car doing, parked at Bexhill?

How quiet the house was with the three children away, she had thought. So she had gone down the lane to the converted barn where her best friend lived. Indeed, she thought now, as her fingers nervously pleated the white net curtain, Edith was her only real friend. The others were mere acquaintances, people she played bridge with or with whom she sat on committees.

Edith had laughed. "So what?" she asked. "Maybe Garth has a girl friend in Bexhill he visits." And then she had laughed still louder. "Oh, pack it up, Mary. I'm only joking. Garth isn't the type to have a girl friend."

"I should hope not," Mary had said sharply, trying to hide her annoyance. Now, thinking, gazing blindly at the sunshine on the grass, she wished, as she had so often done before, that Edith didn't have this vulgar, rather coarse, sense of humour.

She had stayed for lunch and then gone home and found herself thinking again of the Jag. What was it doing in Bexhill? Garth had always parked it at Cooden station.

Standing back, letting the net curtain fall, she tried to smooth out the wrinkles she had made.

If only she hadn't been so obsessed by the fact that she saw the Jag in Bexhill, if only she hadn't given Mrs. Jenkins a lift . . . If only . . . if only . . . if only . . .

Mary turned away from the window

13

and went downstairs. The quietness of the house was oppressive. Everything so clean and tidy, so unlived-in.

She glanced at the clock. Just ten o'clock. Somehow that day, she didn't feel like painting. Nor had she felt like it ever since Garth . . .

Making herself a cup of coffee, she took it to the wide patio, where she was sheltered from the sea breeze and the warmth of the sun could caress her, and began to remember that day again.

Garth had been late coming home that night. He often was and if Mary was at home, she would let Mrs. White go off down the lane to her small stone cottage and her grumpy old husband, and dish up the dinner herself. That night, as every night, Garth read the newspaper as she dished up. For the first time, she had wondered why he didn't read it on the train. Surely most men did?

As she carried the casserole of mushrooms and chicken into the dining-room, she said casually:

"I saw the Jag at Bexhill station today."

The newspaper did not move. Garth's voice came from behind it. "Did you."

He sounded disinterested.

"I thought you always went from Cooden," she said, placing the casserole before him.

He folded the newspaper with his usual slow deliberation and looked up at her.

"I haven't gone from Cooden for ages. I prefer Bexhill," he said as he served her.

"But Cooden's much nearer . . . " She had sat down, taken the plate he passed her and began to eat.

"Is it?" Garth's voice changed. There was a cold note in it. "I happen to prefer it. Isn't that reason enough?"

She tried to smile, a little scared. "Of course, Garth, I . . . I just wondered."

As she ate the meal, Edith's words had pounded in her head.

'Perhaps Garth has a girl friend who lives in Bexhill.'

Looking at him as he silently ate and obviously enjoyed the meal, she told herself that Garth wasn't like that. You could trust Garth.

On the patio, Mary put down her empty cup with a little bang. How naîve she had been!

Anyhow, the seed of doubt had been sown. Maybe she noticed then, but it seemed that Garth was late more frequently in the days that followed. Several times she rang the station and checked the train had been punctual. One night she drove the Mini to Bexhill. At the station, they said the train had come in on time. She drove all over Bexhill, looking for the Jag. At last she found it. Parked in front of a block of flats at the far end of the front.

The next day she had gone to Edith for advice.

"So what?" Edith said. "That proves nothing. It could be a male friend. Or a business acquaintance."

"I have a feeling . . . " Mary said slowly. Her eyes smarted. "How can he do this to me, Edith?"

Edith laughed. "Oh, be your age. Garth's a man. A human being. I must admit I'd be very surprised if it is a girl friend, Mary. After all, I'm quite personable and I've made plenty of passes at him and he's always given me a firm brush-off."

"You — made passes at Garth?" Mary was shocked.

How Edith had laughed. "Of course. Don't you flirt with every attractive man?"

"Not when they're married," she said stiffly.

"My poor innocent child, that's part of living. If he's the faithful type, like Garth, you get a polite brush-off. If he isn't . . . well . . . " She had shrugged her shoulders. "*C'est la vie.*"

After three days Mary had been able to stand it no longer. She drove in her Mini car to Bexhill, parked it in a side road and was waiting at the station when Garth's train arrived. It wasn't difficult to hide herself, with so many people about, taxis and cars.

Garth's head was high above the other men's as he walked out of the station.

He was not alone.

Catching her breath, Mary watched Garth turn to take the woman's arm. Short, rather plump, she wore a well-cut white raincoat and small hat perched on hair that looked grey. Garth helped her into the Jag, walked round and slid behind the steering wheel, laughing at something she had said, and then he drove off.

Mary found it hard to move. But somehow she got to the Mini. Then she drove along the front. Yes! The Jag was parked outside the same block of flats.

She never knew quite how she drove home. Mrs. White was sitting in the rocking chair in the kitchen, happily knitting.

"No phone calls?" Mary asked.

Mrs. White shook her head.

"I've got a migraine, Mrs. White. Could you stay and dish up for Mr. Herron? I don't feel I can face food."

"Of course I can. You hop off upstairs, have a good hot bath and I'll bring you up a nice cuppa. I'll tell Mr. Herron . . . "

"My husband may be late . . . "

"I don't mind, Mrs. Herron. It's comfy sitting here and my old man's down at the pub tonight so don't you fret."

Mary took sleeping pills and was asleep when Garth came to bed. Nor did she see him in the morning for she woke late, this time with a real migraine.

As usual, she fled to Edith for help.

"How can he do this to me . . . " Mary asked the sprawling woman on the couch, so gaudy in her black stretch-pants and orange silk shirt, her hair an unnatural, obviously dyed, red. "We've been so happy."

Edith sat up. "What d'you mean by happiness?"

"Happiness?" Mary fumbled round in her mind. "Happiness. Well, what I felt. Feeling secure. Safe. Knowing that I had Garth . . . that I could trust him . . . that he loved me."

"You poor silly drip. You haven't a clue. What you want is a father not a man . . . Look, suppose Garth has a girl friend, which I doubt for I'm sure there's some logical explanation for it all. But even if he has, he'll grow tired of her. Men usually do. He loves his home, his children and . . . and you. Just be patient."

It was easy for Edith to talk. It hadn't been so easy for Mary to follow this advice. The day before the three children were due home, Mary knew she had to do something.

"Garth . . . " she said abruptly. "Could

you manage to come straight home from the station while the children are here?"

He lowered the newspaper and stared at her.

"Come straight home? But . . . "

"Please don't lie to me, Garth. I know you don't come straight home. You drive that woman to her flat and . . . "

"That woman?" Garth said, his voice furious. "What the hell . . . "

"I don't know her name." Mary glared back at him. After all, he was the one in the wrong. He had no right to be angry.

"Who's been gossiping about me? Your sexy friend, Edith, I suppose, trying to make trouble . . . " His voice was unsteady.

Anger — or guilt? Mary wondered.

"Edith had nothing to do with it. I saw you, Garth."

"You? Snooping . . . ?" Garth rose, towering above her. "I can explain."

She had stood up, too. "I don't want you to. I don't want to discuss it. It's just . . . just that I don't want the children to know . . . " Then she had fled from the room, afraid he would see her tears and despise her for them.

They never did discuss it. Every night, Garth came straight home from the station and spent his usual hour or two with the children, who adored him. He also brought home work to do and when the children were asleep or Voi was watching the television, Garth would retreat to his study, and Mary would go to bed, taking sleeping pills to make sure she was asleep by the time he came up.

It was near the end of the summer holidays that everything blew up. Garth had taken Robbie, who was nearly eight years old, into Bexhill so that they could both get their hair cut. Suzy and Voi had quarrelled all the morning, Mrs. White had a bad cold and was full of her woes about her husband's health, Edith was away, and Mary had felt on edge. This difficult time was slowly gnawing at her nerves. The slightest thing seemed to trigger off her anger.

And Robbie had come running in to show her a set of model vintage cars Garth had bought him. Robbie's hair had been cut too short, almost like a crew cut, Mary noticed, and he was excited ...

"Mum ... we had ice creams afterwards. Daddy met his friend at the barber's. Auntie Carol's got twin sons. They're nine and one's tall and one's short ... and then we all went and had ice creams."

Something exploded in Mary's brain. "Robbie, run and wash your hands ... " she said sharply and the small boy, giving her a startled look, obeyed. He had barely left the room when she swung round to look at Garth.

"How dare you ... " she said, her voice low, shaking with fury. "How dare you introduce my son to that woman ... one of your ... your ... " Edith could have said the word but Mary couldn't.

Garth's face was white. "You believe that? You believe that she ... ?"

"What else can I believe? How could you, Garth? Have you no sense of decency, no loyalty to me ... "

"Mary, I can explain. I offered to but ... "

"I don't want your lies ... "

Then he had caught her by the shoulders. His fingers hurt her. The first

22

time he had ever hurt her. Physically.

"You've got to listen. Carol Stirn and I are friends. Good friends but that's all. She works for the firm. We both happen to travel on the same train so we talk and I give her a lift home. She lives with her mother and her twin sons. She is a widow. Sometimes I have a drink there. You see, her mother goes out a lot and Carol . . . well, she's lonely, too."

She had wrenched herself free. "A likely story! How can I believe that! I won't have my children . . . "

Then he had looked at her strangely. "You don't believe me, do you? Or is it that you don't want to believe me? Is this what you've been working to achieve? Well, you've succeeded . . . " and he had walked upstairs.

Later he came down with a suitcase.

Mary was in the lounge. "We've the children to consider," Garth said. "Think it over," he said curtly and then was gone.

Gone. And he had not come back.

The children had asked questions and she'd had to lie. 'An urgent phone call from London.' 'Daddy had to go at once.' No, she didn't know when he'd be back.

But he had come back. Just once. On the day he knew she had to go to the Red Cross Committee meeting so he must have been sure she wouldn't be there. She never did find out what he told the children exactly. Just some thing about having to go to Paris and Hamburg. But later she had seen his passport in his cupboard and, several times, Voi, seventeen years old and devoted to her father, had behaved oddly, looking at Mary strangely, almost as if she hated her. Had Voi also seen the passport? Mary wondered.

Those last days had been a nightmare. It'll be all right when the children go back to school, Mary had thought.

But it wasn't. It was infinitely worse. For now she was quite alone. Completely deserted. Even by Mrs. White.

The phone bell shrilled. Mary hurried indoors. It was a firm of builders. Apparently the roof needed something doing to it.

"We sent the estimate about three weeks ago, Mrs. Herron. If you want it done before winter . . . " the man, who sounded annoyed, said.

"I'll have to ask my husband . . . " Mary began and then stopped dead. She slammed down the receiver.

Garth

GARTH sat at his desk, signing letters, reading them through quickly. He was the youngest partner of Herron, Kendall and Seale. Although he had inherited his position, he had also earned it by hard work. Educated at Lancing, and Oxford, then he had started at the bottom of the ladder and worked his way up enjoying each step for he liked meeting people and gaining their confidence. Before Frank Herron, Garth's father, died, the firm had been enlarged and admitted two partners, both considerably older than Garth but the three worked in surprising harmony.

His office was the least pretentious of them all, showing Garth's taste for contemporary furniture and art. Only one painting on the wall, an abstract ablaze with impossible crimsons and yellows. Plain white carpet, dark blue curtains, a wide polished satinwood desk, two deep armchairs, his own swivel chair.

The phone bell shrilled. "Who? Put her through at once," Garth said in his deep voice.

In the brief breathing space he had, his long lean face showed surprise and there was a young eagerness in his voice as he greeted his wife. Was she sorry for those things she'd said? he wondered.

"Mary? Yes . . . ?"

Her voice came over the air, impersonal, dutiful as always.

"Garth, the builders rang up about the estimate for the roof. They say you must make a decision soon if you want it done by winter . . . "

He caught his breath. The same Mary!

"I suppose it had better be done," he said, "but just do what you like. It is your house . . . "

"Oh, Garth, it isn't. It's *our* house . . . " she said, her voice faintly accusing. "You know that. It was a gift to us both . . . "

How he had hated that house, from the first time he saw it. 'Mon Repos'! What a name for a five-bed-roomed house. Yet how could they refuse it when it was a well-meaning gift?

Though was it? he often wondered.

Mary thought so but he had his doubts. He had always felt that Mary's parents had given them the house to ensure that their beloved daughter was not going to live too far away from *their* house in Battle. They'd probably discussed the matter with his parents who lived just outside Hastings. Little Common had been near enough for both lots of parents to 'keep a loving eye' on them, and yet far enough away to look as if the old folk were not interfering.

He sighed. "All right, Mary, then phone them to go ahead."

"There are so many things, Garth. Bills coming in and . . . "

"I left cheques . . . "

"But . . . "

"Look, Mary," he said firmly. "Don't worry. Put everything, including the cheques, into a big envelope and send them along to Max Rivers. He'll cope with everything for you."

Max was a good solicitor and a close friend. Maybe Mary could lean on Max now she hadn't got him, Garth thought.

"You all right? Heard from the kids?" he went on, trying to keep his voice casual.

"No, I haven't, but they haven't been gone long." Mary sounded as if she didn't care whether she heard or not, he thought unhappily. "I've had some bad migraines . . . "

"Better see the doctor, then."

"D'you think I ought to, Garth? If you do, I'll make an appointment right away."

"Well, that's up to . . . " he began and then sighed. Mary had never been able to make a decision. "I think it would be a good idea," he said briskly.

"I'll go . . . Oh dear . . . " Mary suddenly sounded distressed. "There's someone at the front door . . . "

"Let Mrs. White go . . . "

"She's gone . . . to London. Her husband's in hospital. The Heart Hospital, I think. Got a thrombosis or something in his leg. I must go, Garth. They're ringing hard . . . "

"Goodbye . . . " he said and replaced the receiver.

He rested his face in his hands, letting his fingers rake through his thick dark hair. Only Mary could behave like this. Acting as if nothing had happened. Had she forgotten their quarrel? Had she dismissed it as a nightmare, a dream she'd never had?

Mary possessed the deft knack of forgetting things she disliked or that disturbed her.

Yet how — oh, good grief, how could he forget the shrill fury in her voice as she accused him of . . .

There was a quiet tap and the door opened. "Mr. Kendall wondered if you could go along and see him right away, sir . . . " Miss Yates, his very efficient secretary, said.

Garth stood up. "Of course. Tell him I'll be right along."

Going to the window, he looked down. Fifteen storeys below the London traffic swirled and weaved through the narrow streets of the City. He rested his hot face for a moment against the glass. Talking of migraines, it looked like he had an outsize headache coming up.

He had heard from the children. A rather sprawly impatiently printed letter from young Robbie, full of the new friend he'd made, whose father lived in South Africa and owned a Game Reserve.

"Dad . . . he says maybe they'll ask me out one hols. Wouldn't that be super? You'd let me go, wouldn't you?"

Robbie and his animals, Garth thought, with amused affection. What would Robbie end up as? Somehow, Garth couldn't see his small son being a stockbroker. Maybe he'd be a Vet. — or, as Robbie's new ambition was likely to be, a Game Warden. His ambitions changed almost daily, being influenced by the friend of the moment.

Garth'd heard also from Suzy. Dear, ambitious, determined little Suzy with her long gangly legs, and her great heart. 'We missed you, Daddy darling, and I hope you won't work two hard and get too tied . . . ' Spelling was not Suzy's strong point which maybe was not surprising for she was brilliant at so many other things, Maths. and oddly enough, Latin.

Suzy could never bear anyone to be hurt. She would fall over backwards to prevent that. Yet she had this strong ambitious streak and her secret, though she shared it with him, ambition was to be another Madame Curie.

'Wouldn't it be wonderful . . . ' she had said, her angular young face, for she was only nine, dreamy; 'to know that you had helped thousands, no, millions of people back to good health? Oh, Daddy, that's what I'd like to do. Then I could die happy.'

They had been walking through the garden and it was late twilight. Somewhere an owl hooted. He had found it hard not to hug her tightly and tell her how much he loved her. Instead, he had said in a matter-of-fact voice: 'I see no reason why your dream shouldn't come true, Suzy. You've got a good brain. The rest is up to you.'

And her face had been radiant. "You really think I have a chance?"

He'd dropped a kiss on her small turned-up nose. "I don't think so, darling. I know it."

Voi's letter had been the only disturbing one. It had been full of a new boy friend, Bob Beeching.

"We never seem to run out of things to talk about, Dad. He's an architect and great fun. Only thing that worries me is that his parents are rather stuffy . . . "

Garth had been amused at first, "Stuffy"? Weren't all oldies 'stuffy' in the eyes of a seventeen-year-old? Wouldn't Bob think that Voi's parents were 'stuffy', too? Then he caught himself wondering about this Bob. What type of fellow would he be? Voi might be seventeen but she was a very young, oddly-immature seventeen. She knew all about the birds and bees, of course. He'd supplied her with books to study and she'd said they taught it in school. He'd wished her mother could have told her, but knew that that was beyond Mary's scope. Poor Mary, who had known practically nothing when she got married.

He shivered suddenly and turned away from the window. Would he ever forget the frightened look on Mary's face on their wedding-night? The plea of weariness . . . the instinctive recoil as he took her in his arms. Her confession that her mother had told her nothing, but that a friend at school had. Poor Mary . . .

It had shocked him to realise that she had been told that this was a part of marriage which had to be 'endured'.

She could not understand that it should give the woman pleasure as well as the man. He had bought books and studied them with her. She had listened, her face blank, but her eyes had shown her disgust. Gradually he had made fewer and fewer demands on her and after Robbie's birth, she had said one night that she felt they'd had enough children and so he had ceased to make love to her. He didn't want a wife who was 'willing'. Knowing she was relieved by his 'neglect' had hurt him still more. Perhaps it started the rift between them that had seemed to grow, because it was about then that she became friendly with Edith Burrows.

He turned away from the window and the roar of traffic, walked down the corridor just past Paul Samuel's office and Carol came out.

"Hi . . . " he said with a half smile.

She smiled back but it was an anxious smile. "Everything all right, Mr. Herron?" she asked. They were always discreet at the office.

"Fine. My wife just rang me."

"Did she?" Carol's eyes lit up. "Then

. . . then you'll be coming down on the train tonight?"

"No. It was about the roof." He gave an odd smile and lowered his voice: "Don't worry. Things'll work out . . ."

Carol did not know the whole truth, just simply that he and Mary had quarrelled and he was staying in London while they sorted things out. He knew Carol missed his companionship on the train. He missed hers. But he had no wish to have her involved and if Mary was capable of snooping, she was more than likely having him followed by a private detective!

He had become friendly with Carol Stirn by chance. But, of course. Mary would never believe that. She didn't want to! It had been on a hot, stiflingly humid, summer's night and the train had been packed with Londoners seeking the cool breezes of the sea. She had sat down next to him in the crowded carriage and had given him a half-smile. Her face had seemed faintly familiar and he must have stared at her with a puzzled look for she said:

"Yes, we have met. I work for your

firm. I'm Mr. Samuel's secretary."

"Of course!" He'd remembered her, then. A quiet girl. He had noticed her several times when seeing Paul. "Paul Samuel. The old tiger. He's been with us for years and is a fine man but . . . "

"His bark is much worse than his bite . . . " she told him quickly and Garth had laughed.

"That's a good one. He looks something like a bloodhound with his mournful eyes and those long hanging jowls. He told me you were very efficient."

How she'd laughed. "I try to be but . . . "

"Have you been with us long?" he'd asked.

"Two years."

They got talking after that and he was rather surprised to find how relaxed he felt. He left the train at Cooden.

On the Monday morning he walked the length of the train until he found her.

"May I?" he said, as there was an empty seat by her side.

"Of course." She smiled at him.

That was how it all began. They

talked. He heard about her twin sons, her mother who lived with her and looked after the boys. He learned that she always hurried from the train home as her mother loved to go out in the evening.

"She's Bingo-crazy," Carol laughed. "But I'm glad she's got such an interest for she hasn't much in life to make her happy."

Nor have you, he'd thought sympathetically. A widow, still in her thirties, and with two boys of nine years old to bring up alone!

When his season ticket expired, he took one out to Bexhill. He was sure he'd mentioned it to Mary but she had probably listened to what he said but hadn't heard. So often Mary had that vague look as if her thoughts were miles away.

So he had started driving Carol home and she'd been most grateful. Rather diffidently offered him a drink. He'd got to know the boys, strangely different for twins, and made friends with the mother, Mrs. Walters. But that was all there was to it.

Admitted, he liked Carol's company, felt relaxed with her. Admitted also, he had realised more and more recently how much he needed companionship. He had tried to talk to Mary but it wasn't easy. That blank look of hers. The dutiful: 'I'm sure you're right, darling, but I wouldn't know.' The inability to argue or to discuss anything, even. The refusal to face up to the facts of life. Her immediate withdrawal from any responsibility or unpleasant happening. He often wondered if she read anything at all. In a way he'd been glad when Edith Burrows turned up and introduced Mary to the joys of painting. It meant she went out more, made friends. Then bridge was another good thing. Surely these new interests, he had felt, would help Mary to find her own personality, to become someone, not just a shadow. That's what she was. His shadow . . .

"My husband says . . . "

"My husband wants me . . . to . . . "

"My husband . . . " "My husband . . . " "My husband . . . " until he could scream.

Couldn't she think for herself for a

change? Couldn't she once say: "I . . . "

He caught his breath. She had. At last. She'd said:

"I don't want your lies . . . "

So it had done something. For once, she'd thought for herself. Or had she? Was she using Edith's words?

Edith Burrows. A gaudily-dressed brash woman, yet with something vaguely sad about her. No one knew much about her. Some said she was man-crazy. She'd encouraged him but had been quick to take the hint that he wasn't interested. Maybe she was trying to help poor Mary. But all her help had done so far was to alienate them. Her encouragement for Mary to play bridge, paint and sit on committees had given Mary a new life — but a life in which a husband had no part.

Sighing heavily, he walked down the corridor to Kendall's office.

When he returned from lunching with Kendall and a prospective client, Garth's secretary told him that his wife had been on the line.

"I said you'd call her."

"Thanks. I will . . . " Garth closed

his office door, pausing for a moment. He wondered what the staff thought of the situation. They knew he was staying at the Woodbury Hotcl, knew that he worked late hours at night, and was at the office early each morning. He had sensed a note of wariness in Kendall's voice. Kendall was rather stuffy and . . .

He sat down and took the phone in his hands. The bell rang for some time before Mary answered.

"Yes . . . ?" she said breathlessly. Would she ever learn, he wondered wearily, to identify herself on the phone?

"I understand you called me, Mary. It's Garth . . . "

"Oh, Garth? Oh, yes, of course. Well, I've just heard from Voi, Garth. It came second post. It seems she's made friends with two girls at the Commercial College and they want to share a flat. She says she hates the hostel, there's no privacy and they can't entertain their friends."

He frowned. "She wants to share a flat with two other girls?"

"Yes. She says most of her friends do it. Apparently it's the recognised thing."

"What d'you think about it?"

"Me?" Mary sounded surprised. "Well, I suppose if all the girls do it, it must be all right. I can't imagine my parents letting me do it but then I never wanted to leave home . . . "

How right you are, Garth thought bitterly. A slow anger was growing inside him. Surely if Mary loved her children, she would be more concerned? Letting a child like Voi, just seventeen, live in a flat with two other girls? How could Mary even contemplate it?

"Personally," he said, his voice suddenly harsh. "I think Voi must be crazy to suggest it. While she's in the hostel, we do know there's someone keeping an eye on her. Entertaining their friends . . . " he said sarcastically. "We all know how that can end. Drinks and then, maybe, drugs."

"Well, Garth, if you feel like that," Mary said, "I'll write and tell her."

"No, don't, Mary," he said quickly. "I'll get in touch with her. I'm certain when I explain how . . . how I feel about it, Voi'll understand."

"Then I can leave it to you?"

Mary sounded relieved.

"Yes. Leave it to me."

They said goodbye. Briefly and politely. Like strangers. Not like two people who'd been married for twenty years and had just had a terrible quarrel.

He replaced the receiver and walked to the window. "Leave it to me . . . " he said silently. That's what he'd been saying since the day he met her.

That day was one he'd never forget. How miserable he'd been! Twenty-one and deeply in love with a girl called Nina Harrow. A lovely girl. He could still remember her high cheek-bones, the way her face changed when she smiled, the husky warmth of her voice, the way she nestled in his arms as they danced. And she'd just rejected him.

For a richer man.

She'd been absolutely honest.

"Garth," she'd said, with realistic-looking tears in her eyes, "I'd much rather marry you but your father's a healthy man and may live for years and Johann Crustel is already nearly a millionaire."

"And twenty years older than you," Garth had said bitterly.

"I know but . . . " and her lovely face had changed as she said angrily: "You can't understand. You don't know what it is to be poor, to wonder if you'll be evicted, if you'll starve. You've always had money. I haven't. I need security."

He'd known then that she had never loved him. She'd been playing the field and if anyone came along the next day who was richer or more decrepit than Johann Crustel, she'd drop Johann like a hot potato and marry the newcomer.

But it had hurt. At twenty-one, one still has ideals. He loved Nina so much, Garth knew that his love for her would never die, that she would be his yardstick, that always he would compare other women with Nina.

To cheer him up his parents had given a tennis party. He'd gone dutifully but reluctantly and they produced this strange girl, Mary.

Later, he decided that they'd done it on purpose, because they felt if he was going to keep falling in love with undesirable gold-diggers, it might be an idea to find him a suitable wife right away.

He'd stared at Mary when he first saw her. She was the antithesis of Nina. Quiet where Nina had been gay, shy where Nina was provocatively bold, soft brown hair as against Nina's bright platinum blonde locks. Mary smiled at him. They played tennis together, and later talked. He was flattered at the way she asked his opinion about everything. And when she seemed so impressed by him. They saw more and more of one another. She restored his deflated ego. Also the knowledge that one day she would inherit even more money than he would, reassured him as to her designs. When he talked of love and marriage she looked scared. Somehow it had made him want to look after her, to protect her from the world she found so frightening.

Sometimes he wondered how any girl could be so shy and unworldly in such an age, but when he learned about Mary's background and education, he understood better. This made him want to protect her still more and probably was the reason he had married her.

But he had loved her. He was sure of that. In a protective way, perhaps, but nevertheless, he had loved her!

Had she loved him? he'd often wondered. When they met her father had been slowly dying — though no one spoke of it — of an apparently incurable disease and Mary, who adored her father and was his shadow, was obviously scared of the future. Had she seen him as a replacement of her father? Garth wondered.

He often wondered if she knew what it was to 'love' anyone. She didn't really love the children. She accepted them as a natural part of a woman's life and did her duty by them. But he had been shocked to find there was absolutely no communication between the children and Mary. Nor did she seem to notice this. He had tried to take her place in the children's lives, sharing their interests, listening to their troubles, trying to help them and, as a consequence, they had grown closer to him than to their mother.

This was another aspect of the case that troubled him sorely. If Mary asked him for a divorce and he provided the necessary evidence, she would be given custody of the children. And he didn't feel she was a good enough mother. Nor did he feel that the children could manage without him.

Or he without them.

He prowled round the room, lighting cigarettes, puffing at them angrily, then stubbing them out.

Why wouldn't Mary believe him? he asked himself angrily. Had he ever given her cause to doubt him?

Where had things gone wrong? Perhaps the first irritation had been soon after they were married. Her dependence on him had assumed absurd proportions. It had been the daily joke at the office.

"Your wife phoned you yet?"

She phoned about the most stupid things. A blocked sink. Mrs. White being late. The postman not coming. Or the butcher hadn't any pork (she always asked him the night before what he'd like for dinner next night!) so would he prefer lamb or veal? He'd begged her not to ring him about such trivial things and she had been very hurt.

"I don't think they're trivial. After all, a man needs plenty of good food to keep well and I want you to enjoy your meals."

The odd thing was that he knew she meant it. Yet she had practically never cooked him a meal. He sometimes wondered if she knew how to boil an egg. If Mrs. White was ill or away, she usually got somebody to stand in for her.

And in the holidays, they invariably had some young woman to help with the children. Once he had protested and Mary had looked hurt.

"It's not that I wouldn't love to look after the children, Garth, but I get so very tired."

Tired! He'd wanted to laugh. How could she get tired when she never did anything? But that was an heritage from her parents. Both had been hypochondriacs and had brought her up with a terror of disease, food poisoning and over-tiredness.

Her attitude towards the children, so apathetic and disinterested, was what worried him most. Had she no maternal feelings for them? No understanding of young people's problems? Was everything all right 'just because other children did it'?

Now Voi. The anger grew again and he walked back to the desk, dialling the number of Voi's hostel. Even as he got a reply, he realised he was a fool. She'd be at the College now.

"She's out, Mr. Herron," a smooth impersonal voice said. "Shall I ask her to call you?"

"No. I'll ring her later. What time do you have dinner?"

"Seven o'clock."

"Thanks . . . " He slammed down the receiver, put his hands in his trouser pockets and went to the window to gaze out moodily. It was all the fault of this new boy friend, of course. Bob . . . oh yes, Beeching. He'd had this bright idea of getting Voi in a flat . . . easy enough to get rid of the other girls and have her alone! Well, Bob had run up against trouble, Garth thought, this was one time the lad would not succeed!

His anger grew as he watched the hands of the clock crawl. Funny how slow time went when you wanted to hurry it up. He could not concentrate on work, his mind kept going back to the past.

Remembering Mary when he first knew her. Her delightful shyness, her frailty, her dependence on him. The hideous house they'd had to accept. His parents' own gift of Victorian furniture. When both lots of parents had died, he'd thought they could move nearer London — for it was a long way to commute daily — and with furniture they'd chosen. But Mary had wept.

She rarely cried, fortunately, in front of him. She knew how much it upset him. It made him angry, too, for his mother had often used tears as a weapon against his father and Garth had hated her for it.

Why should Mary cry, anyhow? She had everything a woman could want. A good husband, a luxurious home, three lovely kids and the faithful Mrs. White.

That reminded him. He sat down at the desk and dialled the hospital. It was good news. Apparently Mrs. White's husband was progressing 'as well as can be expected'. Mrs. White was a good soul, hard-working, efficient and loyal.

He looked at the clock. Not four

o'clock yet. He decided to write to the kids.

Robbie first. Enthusing sympathetically about the possibility of one day flying out to Africa with his friend and staying on the Game Reserve. Thanks be, Garth thought, that Robbie had taken well to boarding school. Garth had been a bit worried. Robbie was young. But he had reacted well and enjoyed the companionship of kids of his own age.

That was one time, Garth remembered, that he had been really angry with Mary.

Garth had got home at his usual time — just after seven o'clock, and there was Robbie, sitting on the patio in the rain, locked out of the house.

The small boy, all alone, had looked painfully vulnerable and Garth had been furious when Mary explained casually later.

"I forgot Mrs. White wasn't going to be there. We were discussing the Fête and . . . well, I just forgot."

She had just forgotten! Just like that. And left a kid of seven years old to come home from school at four o'clock and sit outside on a cold wet day for nearly three hours? Hadn't she ever heard of those lunatics who roam about the coast murdering small children? Hadn't she thought of how a kid of that age would feel, all alone, hungry, wet and cold?

It was then Garth had sent Robbie to boarding school. And it had worked well.

At last it was half-past six and he phoned the hostel.

The same impersonal voice expressed regret. "I'm afraid Voi Herron isn't in tonight. She is having dinner with friends."

Friends!

Garth nearly exploded. "You don't know where . . . " he began and stopped.

He wasn't going to humiliate Voi by acting the angry parent and checking her movements. "Thanks," he said instead. "Would you leave a message for my daughter and ask her to phone me tomorrow. Tell her it's important."

Voi

VOI walked along the Embankment, her hand in Bob's. He smiled down at her and she felt a glow go through her. Never had she felt like this before. This strangely wonderful happiness. He was older than most of the boys she knew. He was twenty-two and she was seventeen. He was fun. They'd danced in a dusky discotheque, their hands touching lightly as they passed one another, his eyes meeting hers and giving that special smile.

The Thames was amazingly still on this warm September night, the lights reflected in the quiet water. But then, everything seemed still, Voi thought. As if they, like her, were waiting. But for what? She had no idea nor was she really curious. She only knew that this was a special moment in her life. Something to be treasured and appreciated.

"I'm glad I met you, Voi," Bob said suddenly. He was thin as well as over six feet tall, and had amazingly long legs. He was wearing a dark suit. Very elegant! She wondered if he'd dressed up to impress her. She hoped so. She had. For him. It was her prettiest frock, chiffon, with a high collar of diamanté and similar cuffs on the long loose sleeves. Blue. The same blue as her eyes, Bob had said. And she had felt her cheeks go red and he had smiled at her. Maybe it was then she knew? She wasn't quite sure when she actually realised that she loved him.

They had met by chance. She had gone to the local library to look up some words for an essay they had to write and had bumped, literally, bumped into him. She had nearly fallen but he had grabbed her in time. As he helped her straighten up, he had apologised.

"It was my fault," she'd said quickly. "I wasn't looking."

"Dreaming?" he'd asked. And then had added: "Of someone?"

How she'd blushed. "No . . . I was thinking of an essay we've got to write. I'm not good at essays."

"I'm sure you're good at everything," he'd said. Gravely. He meant it. She could feel that. "What's the essay about?"

"Ambition . . . and . . . and I haven't any," she'd added dolefully. "How can I write that?"

"You must have some kind of ambition . . . ," he'd said. "Look, couldn't we have a coffee and talk about this?"

They'd sat outside the café, on the pavement, in the sunshine, a rather ragged red sunshade perched above them.

"Ambition is a funny sort of word . . . " he'd said gravely. "I'd suggest you quoted from the dictionary. If I remember rightly . . . " He leaned his head back, closed his dark eyes so she'd had the chance to study his long lean face with the gentle mouth and surprisingly square chin. "Ambition is a desire for honour and fame and power . . . Well, personally . . . " he opened his eyes and smiled at her. "I'm not sure, then, that it's very praiseworthy to be ambitious. I mean, it sounds like Hitler — wanting power and fame."

"I think what people usually mean

is what you're going to do with your life . . . "

"Who can tell? The slightest thing can change everything. I mean, look at us. If we hadn't bumped into one another, we'd never have met, would we?" She blushed. An irritating habit everyone said she'd grow out of. "Ambition . . . what is your ambition? Mine is to be a great architect. Not because I want power or fame but I want to be good enough to make use of all the exciting new ideas being born. I want to build something I'm proud of — something people will look at and never forget." And then he'd smiled.

"What a bore I am. Tell me about yourself. Your ambition — which you say you haven't got. What d'you want out of life?"

"Happiness."

"Fair enough. But who can define happiness?"

Then he'd ordered two more coffees. She didn't want another and she was sure he didn't, either, but she knew it was to postpone the moment of parting and she was glad he'd ordered them.

"One of the definitions of happiness in the dictionary," Bob had gone on, "is contentment. By the way . . . " He gave her the sweetest smile imaginable. "Am I boring you?"

"On the contrary," she said, her voice lilting. "I am fascinated." It was fun talking to him like this, pretending to be the intellectual she was not. "Please go on."

"Well, this essay of yours. You could say you despise the abuse of power, the publicity of fame and that, in other words, you are a normal pretty girl who one day hopes to be happily married and with four children."

She was startled. "How did you know?"

Then he'd held her hand. "I didn't. I was hoping. There isn't . . . isn't anyone yet?"

She shook her head, staring at him. Then he let go of her hand and it felt lonely and cold.

"Maybe we should get down to business," he said with that oddly lopsided smile. "My name is Bob Beeching. I'm twenty-two, I live with my parents near Esher and I am, as I've already told you, an architect. Well?" he waited, looking at her.

"I'm Voi Herron. I'm seventeen. I'm learning shorthand and typing, and languages at the Upton Commercial College."

"An intellectual?"

"Oh no. Not really." She had to laugh. "You see, I don't really want to do *anything*, but I couldn't just do *nothing* so I've simply got to do *something*." She had doodled on the table with her finger, avoiding his eyes. "Not like Mum. I don't know how she can bear it. She just exists. All she does is dabble in painting and play bridge. She doesn't cook or sew or . . . or anything. She never has and she doesn't want to. But that isn't living, that's existing."

"But she's a wife and mother. Isn't that living?" he asked.

She'd looked up at him. "Is it enough? Sometimes I wonder. It might be while the kids are young but we're all away from home."

"Some people are happy doing nothing."

"I couldn't be, so I asked Dad. He's

. . . he's great. I said I'd like to work for him. He's a stockbroker. He advised me to do this. He said that in time my use of languages could let me help him. That's what I'd like to do."

"He's right, you know."

"I know but I do hate shorthand so."

Then she looked at her watch and leapt to her feet in horror. "I'll be late. Mr. Leale who takes this class is an absolute beast . . . "

Bob walked with her to the College and asked her if they could meet again.

"If you like to," he added.

And she looked up at him, getting a crick in her neck. And she said the most truthful thing she had ever said.

"You know I'd like to . . . " and then her face and neck had burned with embarrassment.

Bob hadn't seemed to notice for his face was one great big beam. "I'm glad."

They'd met the next night, and the next, and the next. Tonight he'd asked her out to dinner and they'd walked and talked and now it was time to go back to the Hostel, as they were very strict about curfew hours.

He hailed a taxi and they sat very close together, his arm round her shoulder gently. She rested her head against his arm.

"It's been a lovely evening, Bob."

"We'll have many more lovely evenings, Voi . . . " he said gently, and traced her nose and eyebrows with his finger. "Voi . . . " and then he closed his mouth for a moment. "Voi, I'd like to meet your parents."

She shivered happily. "I'd like you to meet them. Dad's away. He's . . . he's in France or Germany on business but when he comes back . . . "

"Good. My parents are . . . well, they're okay but . . . well, they're rather old, Voi. I was the after-thought. My brother is twelve years older than me. They're . . . well, they're rather stuffy. We live near Esher and they're very conventional and rather Victorian in outlook. But they're all right . . . "

She smiled at him "I'm sure they are . . . "

He left her at the Hostel, lightly kissing her, arranging to meet her the next evening.

And she went into the rather dismal hall. On the notice-board she looked for letters. There were none. Just a note. She opened it quickly.

"Message from your father. Please ring him tomorrow. It's important," the note said.

Voi's happiness fell off her like a cloak discarded. What could be 'important'? So he wasn't in France or Germany? Then it had been his passport she saw in the wardrobe? So he'd lied . . . and so had Mum. But why?

Walking upstairs to her minute room, Voi's feet dragged. It could only mean . . .

Her mind shied away from the word.

Hers was a small room with a divan, a wardrobe and a chest of drawers and a chair. She undressed quickly in the dark, for if one of her friends saw a streak of light under the door, they'd drop in and then they'd make coffee and sit and talk and . . . and she didn't feel like talking.

She brushed her shoulder-length fair hair one hundred times. Bob said her hair looked like ripe corn and felt like silk! Then she cleaned her teeth and scrambled into bed.

But she couldn't sleep. If there was a . . .

She closed her eyes and then opened them wide in dismay. Bob had said his parents were 'stuffy'. That meant they would strongly disapprove of . . .

Waking late, she had to scurry through dressing and rush down for breakfast and then to the College. She rang her father in the first break.

"Voi . . . I tried to get you last night and you were out." He sounded annoyed, almost accusing.

"I didn't know you were in London, Dad . . . " she attacked in self-defence.

She heard him sigh and her heart sank. "No, you didn't. You're right. Voi, I want to talk to you. Very seriously. Are you free for lunch?"

Her heart sank still farther. "Yes, Dad."

"Good. Meet me at the Rainbow Restaurant sharp at one."

"Yes, Dad."

The morning both crawled and flashed by, which didn't make sense, and yet it did, for she both wanted to see her father and dreaded it. She didn't want him to put it into words for then it would make it the truth.

Exactly one minute late, she found he was waiting. She ran to him, her hair swinging, and hugged him.

"Oh, Daddy, it's so good to see you . . . "

His face was grave as he kissed her. "We've a lot to talk about, Voi," he said and her momentary happiness vanished.

He let her choose and then he ordered lunch. Offered her a cigarette, looked pleased when she refused, and lit one for himself.

"Voi . . . " he began and she waited, frozen with fear. "About this idea of sharing a flat . . . "

She stared at him.

"A flat?"

He frowned. "Yes. You wrote to your mother, saying you wanted to share a flat with two other girls . . . "

"Oh, yes . . . Of course, I forgot. Yes . . . " she said, her words jumbled as she fought the desire to laugh. She was so relieved she wanted to get up and dance and sing. How wrong she'd been . . . he only wanted to talk about the flat!

"I've changed my mind, Dad . . . " she told him and was surprised at the instant relief on his face. "You see, I talked it over with Bob and he doesn't think it's a good idea."

"He doesn't?" her father sounded rather surprised.

"No. He says three girls might seem good friends but when it comes to sharing chores, well, he says then comes trouble. You usually get a lazy one and one who forgets to pay her way. And . . . and he says that my girl friends might not have the right type of boy friends . . . " Voi hesitated. "He said he didn't mean to sound pompous and a prig but I am rather young and . . . "

Her father's eyebrows went up. "He said that?"

"Yes. Oh, Dad, he's very . . . well, protective. He says I'm very immature and . . . " She smiled. "Oh, Dad, I'm longing for you to meet him and he wants to meet you."

Her father was laughing. "That makes two of us. How about tonight? Have dinner with me?"

"Oh, that'd be lovely. I'm meeting him

at half past six at the Cat Inn."

"Good . . . "

It was as they were having coffee and she had one eye on the clock, for it was her Russian lesson that afternoon and she didn't want to miss it with exams at the end of the term, she suddenly remembered something. Dad was in such a good mood that she took a chance.

"Dad, I knew you hadn't gone to France or Germany for I saw your passport."

He looked a bit uncomfortable. "No, Voi. I'm afraid I lied."

"Why?" She clenched her hands tightly under the table.

"Your mother and I had a bit of a misunderstanding so I thought I'd give her a few days to think things over."

"Think things over . . . ?" Voi said fearfully.

"She . . . well, she accused me of doing something and when I explained, she refused to believe me. I thought . . . well, I thought, give her time to think about it and she'd know that I'd told her the truth."

"You're not . . . not going to have a . . . a divorce?"

He looked at her gravely. "I hope not, Voi. It's up to your mother."

"Oh, Mum won't want one . . . " Voi said quickly. "She needs you too much, Dad. Why, she's always quite lost when you're away from home."

"I know. Sometimes I think she depends on me too much."

"But isn't that what husbands are for? I mean, to be there when you need them?" Voi asked.

She saw her father's eyes twinkling. "There are other reasons for having a husband . . . "

"I know . . . " she said, and realised she meant it.

Husbands were there for you to love — for you to look after and care for, to enjoy being with, to have fun sharing things. Husbands were there . . . well, they were there because you loved them.

As her father led the way outside, hailed a taxi and paid the driver before helping Voi in, he smiled at her from the pavement.

"Know something, Voi? I'm looking

forward to meeting your young man."

All the afternoon as Voi battled with Russian, her mind kept wandering off. She wished there was some way of warning Bob that her father was meeting them but there wasn't. Still, she needn't have worried for Bob was early and looked as smart as he had done the night before.

The Cat Inn was actually in a basement, lit with candles that flickered and with music booming and a few couples dancing on the small floor. Voi was a bit worried about her father's reactions but he seemed to like the place and sat down with a smile and said:

This is on me, don't forget . . . "

He and Bob hit it off at once, Voi saw. Another weight was lifted off her shoulders. She'd hoped they would but some fathers are funny about their daughters' boy friends. But Dad wasn't. She wondered how her mother would react. She'd always seemed to accept their friends, neither liking nor disliking them. Perhaps the word would be 'tolerating' them.

After dinner, her father said he had

to go but he'd enjoyed the evening. "Dad . . . " Voi said quickly. "I was wondering if . . . well, if perhaps we couldn't all three go down to Little Common for the weekend? I mean, before it gets to be really cold down there."

He looked at her gravely and hesitated for only a moment. "An excellent idea. I'll phone your mother and make all the arrangements . . . " He turned to Bob. "If that's all right for you, Bob?"

Bob nodded. "I'd like to very much, sir."

"When can you get away? D'you work Saturdays?"

"Sometimes but I can arrange to have this Saturday off."

"Good. Well, I'll meet you two at the hostel at eleven o'clock and we'll drive down, having lunch on the way. Okay?"

Voi smiled at him. "Oh, Dad, that's super . . . "

She began to think quickly about clothes. She'd buy herself one of those new knickerbocker suits. She'd seen some very smart ones . . . and maybe Saturday night, they'd find somewhere to dance. Then she remembered that her parents were not on speaking terms. But they must bc, if Dad could just phone her like that. Perhaps everything was all right and Mum had already made up the quarrel . . . ?

Her father stood up and Bob stood up, too. He was taller than Dad but much much thinner. He looked like a bean pole next to an oak. But they had the same long lean faces, the same kind of dark hair, slightly receding on the temples, the same full kind mouth . . .

She drew a long deep breath. Oh, how lucky she was, she thought, as she said goodbye to her father and watched him walk away and Bob turned to her with a smile:

"Shall we dance . . . ?"

★ ★ ★

It was raining on Saturday morning but Voi had bought a new blue raincoat and a small souwester hat to match and was wearing her new knickerbocker suit that was also blue, and long white boots.

68

Bob joined her, wearing a cream shirt and dark brown corduroy trousers and jacket, and a duffle coat with a crazy cap pulled down over one side of his head. They stood in the doorway of the hostel, holding hands as they waited.

The black Jag swung round the corner and stopped outside the door. Her father waved to them and Bob picked up their two cases and they raced through the rain to the car.

Voi sat between the two men. She loved it when the jolt of the car pushed her from one arm to the other. She thought her father looked worried so she asked:

"How did Mum take it?"

He grinned. "Well, you know how she takes everything. In a bit of a flap. Mrs. White hasn't been working for her lately, her husband was in a London hospital, so your mother had a panic. However, I managed to trace Mrs. White down and she's gone back for the weekend."

"I expect Mum misses her . . . "

"I bet she does . . . " Her father was silent as he negotiated a passage through the heavy traffic and Voi turned to Bob.

"Did your parents mind you coming?"

He grinned down at her. "They know better. Besides when I told them about what a nice girl you were and all that . . . ! Mum has been matchmaking ever since I was a tiny tot . . . "

Voi's cheeks burned. It was the first time Bob had said anything like that. Did it mean he was . . . well, serious?

She glanced at him sideways quickly and saw that he was looking at her, not smiling, his face grave. Then he took her hand in his and held it tightly.

It had stopped raining by the time they had lunch at a wayside hotel. Voi noticed that her father was rather tense and she began to wonder if it was wise, bringing Bob down at this stage. Suppose Mum was still angry with Dad? But what could Dad have done — or what could Mum think Dad had done — to make her so angry? It wasn't like Mum to lose her temper. Sometimes she was edgy and snapped at them but . . .

As they drove down to Little Common, the sun came out.

Dad glanced across Voi's head at Bob. "As an architect you will moan when you see Mon Repos . . . "

Bob looked at him. "What . . . what did you say its name was?"

Voi's father grinned. "Mon Repos. Makes one want to vomit. My wife's parents gave us the house as a wedding present and we've been landed with the white elephant ever since."

"Don't you like the house, Dad?" Voi asked, startled.

"I hate it . . . " he said with a violence that surprised her. "Always have done. But what can you do with a gift from loving parents?" His voice was sarcastic.

"Why don't you sell it?"

"Your mother loves it."

"Oh . . . " Voi stared at him. It surprised her — somehow home had always been home, she'd never thought of it as an ugly or a beautiful house. Just as home.

"The furniture, too, is ghastly," her father went on. "A gift from my parents. If only parents would mind their own business when their children get married and leave them to live their lives as they want to . . . "

The bitterness startled Voi still more.

She stared at her father's face. It looked as if cut out of stone. She glanced quickly at Bob and saw that he, too, was looking at her father.

"Your parents didn't?" Bob asked gently.

"They most certainly did not. They meant well. At least I imagine so. But they wanted us here, under their eyes. One family lived in Battle, the other at Hastings. My wife had a long empty day with me commuting to the City and she spent most of the first years of our marriage visiting one or other of the families and they practically ruled our lives. When Voi gets married, I only hope her husband has the good sense to take her several hundreds of miles away so that she can be free of the yoke . . . "

"The yoke, Dad?" Voi said uncertainly.

He grinned at her. "The yoke of childhood, Voi. When a woman marries, she should forsake her parents and consider her husband. She should throw off old habits and take on the new — be a person, not a shadow . . . "

"Ah . . . here we are . . . " Voi said gladly as the wrought iron gates appeared before them. How relieved she was! She knew her father had been speaking about her mother. Was that what he thought — that Mum had never thrown off the yoke of childhood? In a way, he was right for Mum was like a child, turning to Dad for everything. But then didn't men *like* that? Didn't it make them feel masculine and important?

"It's not so bad, sir," Bob was saying.

Voi looked at the house as if for the first time. A big red-bricked house with a small turret at either end. Shining windows, all those on the first floor were shrouded with white net curtains. The garden looked bright with chrysanthemums and some dahlias.

The front door opened as the Jag parked by the garage and Mrs. White came out in her blue frock and white apron. She looked agitated.

"Oh, you're earlier than we expected, Mr. Herron. I think Mrs. Herron is still with Mrs. Burrows. She went there for lunch. I'll just slip down and tell her."

Voi's father got out of the car and stretched himself.

"Don't fret yourself, Mrs. White," he

said, borrowing one of Mrs. White's favourite expressions. "I'll stroll down and tell her myself." He turned to Voi. "You show Bob around. We'll be up later on. Okay?"

Something made Voi move to his side, to slip her hand into his and squeeze it. "Okay, Dad, and . . . and thanks a ton . . . " she said quietly.

He smiled down at her understandingly. "Not to worry," he said with equal quietness. "All's going to be well," he said and walked down the lane to Mrs. Burrows little house.

It was fun being alone with Bob. Showing him over the house. The basement where Dad had made a playroom for them, with table tennis, darts, Robbie's electric train, and Suzy's dolls. Her mother's studio with a few paintings turned facewards towards the wall. Her father's study, small and businesslike, the long lounge that ran the width of the house so that they always got sun at some part of the day, the dining-room with its dark mahogany furniture. She discovered that Bob was, like her father, not enamoured of Victorian furniture. This was rather disappointing but couldn't be helped.

When she saw her parents walking up the garden, she knew a moment of fear. But it was all for nothing for the day passed pleasantly, the sun shining, the breeze pleasantly refreshing, the food delicious as only Mrs. White could cook it, the whole atmosphere relaxing and pleasant. It was only on Sunday that trouble began.

Voi sensed it at breakfast. As usual her mother had it in bed but Voi noticed how quiet her father was, how little he ate. Later, when her mother came downstairs, there was a distinct aura of disapproval. If she spoke to anyone, even to Bob, Voi heard this note of condemnation in her mother's voice. As if they had all done wrong and she could not forgive them. It was an unpleasant feeling and it ruined any attempt to regain the pleasant atmosphere of the day before. Several times Voi glanced anxiously at Bob and saw that he, too, had noticed the tension.

So she was not very surprised when Bob told them that he had to go home that night.

He explained with painstaking care, "You see, I'm going out to this estate with the boss and he's a stickler for punctuality, so I must get there early."

"Naturally," Voi's mother said, her voice stiff, "You must put your employer's demands first. We quite understand."

Voi saw her father begin to speak and then stop. "What a pity, Bob, but it can't be helped. We'll look up a train and drive you in to Bexhill," he finally said.

"Why not Cooden station?" Voi's mother asked, her voice icy. "It's nearer."

And then Voi had seen her father swing round, his face angrier than she had ever seen it. "Because I prefer Bexhill, Mary. I've told you so."

She had glared back. "If you . . . " and then she had turned and walked out of the room. There had been an unhappy embarrassed moment of silence, broken by Voi.

"You'd better pack," she said miserably.

She longed to go with Bob, to run from this house full of hate and anger, but she couldn't leave her father. She stared at him, standing there so still, his face expressionless like a closed book. If he was left alone with Mum . . . anything could happen.

At the last moment, Voi decided not to go with them to the station. She wanted a chance to be alone with her mother.

"It's been terrific, Voi," Bob said and held her hand tightly but she wondered if he meant it. "I'll be in touch with you. I may have to go up to Manchester next week."

Managing a smile, she watched the car drive away. Then she turned, her feet dragging, to go into the house.

Was this a polite brush-off? she wondered. Would she ever see him again? Or had he, too, felt the animosity, the threat of destruction of her parents' marriage?

Her mother had gone to sit by the window, getting out cards for her favourite game of patience.

"A nice boy," she said, not looking up. "Are you going steady?"

Voi stood still, holding her hands before her tightly.

"I thought so. I'm not sure — now."

Her mother looked up. "What d'you mean?"

"I mean, after . . . after the way you behaved today . . . "

Her mother frowned. "I don't understand."

"Why are you so angry with Dad?"

Voi saw the flush in her mother's cheeks. "That's no business of yours."

"It is. I'm your daughter. Anything to do with you is my business." Voi took a step forward. "Are you going to divorce Dad?"

She saw the shock on her mother's face. "Does he want me to?"

"I asked him. He said he didn't but that it was for you to decide. He said you won't believe him . . . "

Her mother stood up. "Of course I don't. He's been lying to me all the time. How can I trust him again?"

"What did he do?"

She watched the colour surge over her mother's face and back as she turned away. "I don't want to talk about it."

"But Mother, you must . . . " Voi walked round to face her mother. "What did he do? Was he . . . was he . . . "

Her mother looked at her. "Yes, he was."

"He denies it?"

"Yes. He's lying, of course."

"Why . . . 'of course'? Dad's not a liar . . . "

"That's what I thought . . . "

"And you don't believe him?"

"I can't, Voi — Oh, how can you understand. A child like you. Twenty years and . . . and then he can do this to me." She stopped and, for a moment, Voi was afraid her mother was going to cry.

"So you're going to divorce him?" Voi's voice was dead, lifeless. "You're going to break up the family, spoil everything just because you don't believe Dad. I do. I don't think he'd lie. I know he wouldn't . . . " Her voice began to rise angrily. "If Dad did wrong, he'd tell the truth. Face the consequences. He's not a coward . . . "

Her mother sat down on the couch. "You want to believe him . . . "

"Mother . . . " Voi's voice was stilted, unnatural. "I'll tell you something. If you divorce Dad, you'll lose us all. We'll all go to Dad. Even if the judge says you can have us, we'll run away again and again until he has to give us to Dad . . . "

"Your father can do wrong yet you'd go to him. That's how much love for me you have."

Voi thought how pale her mother looked.

"It has nothing to do with love. Dad needs us. You don't. You need Dad. Not us. You've never needed us. We know that. But Dad needs us. Badly. We couldn't ever hurt him."

"I've always been a good mother . . . "

"Have you? I don't think so. Dad's been father and mother, too. I can tell him anything. You don't listen when I tell you things. Oh, yes, you listen but you don't hear. Think it over. If you divorce Dad, you'll lose us all. Then you'll have no one. No one . . . " Her voice suddenly broke and, terrified she was going to cry, Voi turned and ran, slamming the door behind her, stumbling up the staircase, slamming her bedroom door, locking it, throwing herself down on her bed.

Mary

MARY walked down the lane to the converted barn just before lunch. If Edith Burrows stifled a sigh, Mary didn't hear it. She was far too upset.

She stood in the doorway, looking round the one large room and saw Edith turn from her easel, palette in hand, her paint-smeared smock hanging loosely on her thin body.

"I suppose you're going to tell me it's all my fault, too . . . " Mary said angrily. "I'm sick and tired of hearing . . . of hearing . . . "

Edith moved fast. "Sit down and relax. Kick off your shoes and I'll get us both a drink . . . " she said, almost pushing Mary into a deep chair.

In ten minutes Mary could talk more coherently.

"I took the bills and things to Max, Edith, and . . . and he practically threw me out. As well as practically telling me I was a moron."

"Max?" Edith began to laugh. "He isn't that type. You must be having hallucinations."

"I am not! I never have liked him. When he looks at me, I feel he's mentally undressing me . . . "

"A compliment," Edith murmured.

"I don't see it that way." Mary gave her an angry look. "Today he was . . . well, positively hostile. He took the papers and said of course he could cope, that any child of sixteen could, if she tried. I asked him if he'd heard from Garth. He said no. He imagined that Garth was waiting for my solicitor to write him. So Garth must have told Max all about it, Edith. It's quite obvious that Max is on Garth's side."

Edith took off her smock, straightened her short grey skirt and white shirt, and relaxed. This, she knew, was going to be a long business. She sprawled on the wide divan, pushing the many different coloured cushions up behind her back.

"So?"

"So . . . I asked him what I should do . . . what he thought I should do and

. . . and he said see my own solicitor. He said he wasn't in a position to advise me but if he was, he'd tell me to forget the whole thing, write Garth an apology and start again . . . As if . . . as if I . . . I . . . was in the wrong, Edith," she finished, her face flushed with anger.

Edith swallowed her drink, jumped up to refill the glasses.

"Are you going to?"

"Me . . . apologise? For something he did? Are you out of your mind?"

"Sometimes I think you are, Mary. After all, it is only conjecture on your part . . . "

Mary waved the brandy glass wildly. "That's what he said . . . I went . . . I don't mean Max. I mean I didn't have a solicitor and I told Max so and then he suggested I went to Mr. Angel, he was my father's. So I went and told him everything. He said I had no grounds for divorce . . . but I don't want a divorce, Edith. I want . . . "

"Garth to crawl on his stomach, kiss your feet, and humbly confess? Is that what you want?" Edith asked. "What *do* you want?"

"I don't know . . . I don't know. Mr. Angel asked me if I had any proof of adultery. If I'd had Garth followed by a private detective. I was shocked. I ask you, Edith, how could I do that?"

"You followed him. You snooped . . . "

"That's what old Mr. Angel said, Edith. I said it was quite different. He said I was splitting hairs."

"He's so right . . . "

"But it is different. Can't you understand?" Mary got up and began to walk round the room. She was wearing a too-long brown suit, her stockings were slightly wrinkled and her shoes needed polishing.

"Well, Mary, you must want something? You don't want a divorce, you don't want to humiliate Garth. What do you want?"

Mary stood still, suddenly looking very young and frightened. Like a child, lost, not knowing which way to turn.

"I want to be able to trust him. If he hadn't lied . . . "

"You've no proof that he did lie."

"I saw the woman . . . "

"He explained that friendship."

"Explained! All lies . . . " Mary sat down abruptly, and gulped down more brandy than she normally did, and choked and coughed.

"The whole thing rests, it seems to me," Edith said, quietly, matter-of-factly, "on the fact that you feel unable to believe Garth. Why?"

Mary sighed. "I don't know. I just don't know. I have a feeling . . . "

"So you're prepared to wreck your marriage because you have a 'feeling' . . . What about the children?"

"That's another thing, Edith. Voi blames me."

"Voi knows about it?"

"Apparently! I didn't say anything so don't glare at me. You remember Garth said Voi wanted us to meet this wonderful new boy friend? Well, he seemed quite nice but suddenly, yesterday, he decided he had to go back to town at once. They'd already decided to drive up early this morning. Garth said he'd write a note to Voi's College as to why she was late . . . Well . . . well . . . " Mary paused, looking at her hands, looking in the glass of brandy, anywhere but at Edith.

"Well?" Edith said firmly.

"Well, he said he'd drive Bob to Bexhill and . . . and I said why not Cooden and . . . Garth said he preferred Bexhill . . . and then, well, I was so angry I couldn't speak so I walked out of the room. When they'd gone Voi came and . . . made a most unpleasant scene . . . "

"I'm not surprised . . . " Edith murmured.

"Voi said . . . she said it was all my fault, Edith. She said that . . . that if there was a divorce, she and the others would go with Garth. She said that they'd run away if the judge gave me custody. She said Garth needed them. That I didn't. She said that I was to think about it — that if I divorced Garth, I'd lose them all. I ask you, Edith, my own children . . . " Mary's voice was a wail.

"She didn't mean half of it, Mary. She was upset at the scene. Enough to frighten any lovesick lad off matrimony. She was probably mad at you. One always hurts the one you love . . . "

"Then . . . then you think perhaps she does love me but . . . "

"I'm sure she does. You are, remember, her mother."

"Well, then, what does she . . . what do you all expect me to do? Just act as if this has never happened? Just pick up the bits and go on as before? Is Garth to go on having his girl friend . . . being late for dinner, lying to me . . . "

Edith sighed. "No."

"No?" Mary was startled. "But . . . "

"Because it would never work. So long as you're convinced that Garth lied to you, you can't pick up the bits. You see you might be able to forgive but you'll never be able to forget. Or let him forget. The way you leapt on him yesterday proves that. Why shouldn't he prefer Bexhill to Cooden? That isn't a crime. And he probably did tell you and as usual you listened, but didn't hear."

"Then . . . then what should I do?" Mary almost wailed. "I don't want a divorce, I don't want to lose my children, I . . . "

"Take a holiday right away and think things over."

Mary leaned forward. "That's what old Mr. Angel said." She remembered the funny, bald little man's face as he looked at her. "He told me to go away for six months and think things over."

"There you are, then. Two of us have advised that. You may see everything in a different perspective, Mary. You may realise that you love Garth too much to risk losing him."

"But where on earth could I go?"

Edith jumped up. "I'll toss us up a couple of omelettes. Here . . . take a look at the paper." She threw the newspaper over. "Why not look at the adverts for winter holidays. Go in search of the sun," she said, and walked out to the small built-on annexe which housed the minute kitchen and the even smaller bathroom with its shower.

"Go in search of the sun . . . " Mary echoed as she idly turned the newspaper's pages. She had to smile at the inviting, almost seductive advertisements. Last winter had certainly been pretty miserable, with fogs and then heavy winds, rain and some bitterly cold days. If Mrs. White was going to be difficult! Then there was the central heating of the house, if Garth wasn't there to keep an eye on it, it was pretty temperamental and she hadn't a clue, Mary thought worriedly.

She half-closed her eyes, imagining the big cold house in which she would move about alone, and she shivered. If she had to wait six months before . . . well, it would certainly be nicer to spend those six months in warm sunshine.

Edith came in, the trays balanced neatly in her hands.

"Well, does it appeal?" she asked cheerfully.

Mary nodded. "You think I should go?"

Edith stifled a sigh. "Look, Mary, you're going to be pretty miserable here this winter, aren't you? Things won't improve, they'll actually get worse. You'll become bitter. Resentful. That won't help things. You should go right away, meet new people, and . . . and grow up . . . "

"Grow up?" Mary began to laugh. "I am nearly forty, you know."

"Years don't mean maturity," Edith began and then chuckled. "Hark at me talking! Seriously, Mary, you're still a child. Still the sheltered obedient docile little girl of your elderly possessive parents."

When they had finished, she took both trays and vanished in the kitchen. Mary gazed at the advertisements of huge liners moving leisurely through blue water with a cloudless sky and the sun beaming happily. She never had been on a cruise. It might be fun. When they'd gone on holidays, it was always by car, usually to Cornwall with the kids, staying at Jenny Richards' house which she lent them most years. This year they hadn't gone. Jenny needed the house, she'd written, and somehow they'd left it too late to book in anywhere else. Once, Garth had taken her abroad, to Paris, Vienna and Rome. But they'd flown.

Edith came back with two cups of coffee and settled herself on the divan, clasping her knees, slowly rocking as she talked:

"Can you take the truth, Mary? It's not your fault, not really. It's your parents'. You were unlucky enough to be the only child of elderly parents who not only adored you but devoured you. You've always had it easy, been spoiled. You've grown up to be an egoist with no idea what makes other people tick." She lifted one hand. "Don't interrupt or I'll lose the thread. It isn't your fault, Mary, but you're out of this world. You should have lived in the Victorian age. You've always had someone to lean on. First your father, then Garth. Now me. It isn't good for you. You'll never be a real person until you lean on yourself. Life is lonely. Hard. You have to fight for things you want. Otherwise you don't appreciate them."

She paused. "I used to envy you so, Mary. You had everything a woman could want. I'd have given anything in the world to have a husband like Garth. To have children like yours. You also had good health and money. Everything. Yet now I'm sorry for you. Because you've got nothing. Nothing at all. To live you must love. You've never known what love really is. You think it is something you are given automatically, that it is your right to be loved. It isn't, you know. Love is something you must earn. Often the hard way . . . "

She began to twist the tassel of an

orange cushion. "I've never told you, Mary, but I've divorced three husbands. Each time it broke my heart. Divorce isn't pleasant. It's the most heartbreaking, gruelling experience imaginable. Each time I married I thought this must be real love, the real thing. It wasn't. They grew tired of me. I'm proud. I can't accept humiliations gracefully. So I divorced them and now? I'm forty-six and alone. I've got no one. Nothing! But I'm a person. I paint. I like people. I have interests. But what'll happen to you if you let this 'feeling' of yours ruin your marriage? You've never walked into a hotel alone, have you? You've never coped with income tax or rates. You've always had a man to look after you."

Mary jumped to her feet. Suddenly, it was too much. Everyone blamed and criticised her! "Honestly, Edith, I don't know what you're getting at. I'm sorry about your unhappy marriages. I suppose that's my fault, too. You blame my parents for this yet they loved me. I'm beginning to think they were the only people who did."

She turned and ran, out into the

sunshine, up the narrow rutted lane, home. She looked up at the house for a moment. Garth had never liked it. Nor had she, very much, but it was a gift, and she'd been taught to accept gifts, however much she disliked them, graciously. Besides her parents had loved her and wanted her near them. With her father growing weaker day by day . . .

Running into the house, she snatched up the car key and her handbag. Going to the Mini, reversing, she drove down the road.

She reached Battle and saw that the house was just the same. She pulled up outside the wide gates and looked across the road at it. A big unwieldy house, but they'd had several old servants who stayed with them until her father's death, and her mother's which was less than a month later.

Now the house was a boarding-house, or perhaps it should be called a private hotel. All the windows were open to the autumnal sunshine. It looked the same and yet different. Funny to think she'd been born there, had governess after governess, for her father was very particular, then she had gone to a small private school. Looking back, she realised that she had been a lonely child yet never unhappy for her father had spent a great deal of time with her. She'd had few friends. She rarely got asked out, for her parents hadn't liked any of the girls she'd taken home. Mary smiled tenderly. Bless them, they had thought no one good enough for her.

That reminded her of Jeremy.

Her first love. If you could call the short, slightly ridiculous affair, a 'romance'. Jeremy was a young architect. That's funny, she thought, looking at the leaves of the beech trees ruffling in the wind. They had once been her father's joy! Voi's latest boy friend, Bob, was an architect, too.

Mary had met Jeremy by chance. She'd missed a bus home and was flapping nicely, as Garth would have put it, because her father would be worried, when Jeremy, tall, thin, and red-headed, had pulled up in his M.G. sports car and asked if he could give her a lift. She'd hesitated but he'd had a friendly smile and she didn't want to upset her father so she'd accepted it. Father, of course, hadn't liked him. But then, she remembered, as she put up her hands to her hair, coiled in a knot that threatened to fall in the breeze, her father hadn't really liked Garth. Would he have liked anyone? she wondered.

Anyhow, Jeremy had liked her and had asked her to a dance. Oh, the arguments and tears about it but in the end, Mary had been firm. It was her first and only revolt. Other girls went to dances so why couldn't she? Her father had insisted on driving her to the dance and then fetching her, and she had been furious with him. But Jeremy had understood.

"If you were my daughter," he'd said. "I'd lock you up in the top of a tower, with a guard to keep you safe."

In the end, it had all fizzled out. As her parents had said, it wasn't fair to young Jeremy, just starting his career, to saddle him with a wife. So they had drifted apart. Then her father had grown thinner and weaker and there had been an atmosphere of fear in the house and perhaps that made her see how very old her parents were. The thought frightened her a little but her mother had been forty-eight when Mary was born.

It was at this time that she met Garth who seemed so protective and reassuring.

"H'm . . . " A discreet cough startled her from her memories. Mary turned her head and a policeman was by her side, staring through the open window. "Car trouble, miss?"

"No . . . ," Startled, Mary spoke rather sharply.

"Waiting for someone, miss?" he asked.

"No . . . I . . . " Something clicked in Mary's mind. She must look odd, sitting here, staring into space. She smiled. "No, just remembering the past. I was born in that house . . . "

His plump, reddish face relaxed. "I understand, miss. A little nostalgia, eh? Only, miss, you're not supposed to park like this on a busy road. It's not a good idea you know, miss, looking back."

Puzzled, she stared up at him.

"I know what I'm talking about, miss," he went on. "You look back and it seems it all was perfect. Then you go to the place and everything's the same and yet it isn't for now you can see that it wasn't perfect, after all. I bet, looking at that house, you can remember times when you wept your eyes out miserably, when it was like a prison to you. It happened to me. I was always talking about the place I was born and in the end the missus got fed up and took me back. It gave me a jolt all right and she hasn't heard a word of complaint out of me since." He smiled at her. "Don't sit and dream too long, miss."

"I won't," she promised.

There was something in what he'd said, she realised. Looking back down the years, she saw what a narrow over-protected life she'd led. Edith was right. She had been possessed by love. She'd leaned on her father and then on Garth, always trying to please them, doing what they said without argument. Could you imagine Voi meekly living the life she'd led? Mary wondered. But then Voi had a different temperament.

Mary switched on the ignition, got into gear and drove towards Hastings. About six miles outside the town, she turned off, down a narrow curving road to a small valley. She did not drive down to the house which was now a boarding-school but parked off the road, under a copse of larches. Already some of the leaves were turning colour, she thought, looking down at the big house hemmed in by massive trees.

She had come here to play tennis and had met Garth. At once she had liked him. He made her feel safe. It was a wonderful feeling.

Garth had been wonderful, she thought, her hands clutching the steering wheel. He'd looked after her, given her courage and strength, solved her problems.

And now, that had all gone.

Because she could not believe him.

She turned the car and drove back to Little Common. The blue sky had vanished and low dark clouds were piling up overhead, the late afternoon surprisingly ominous. How still the house was as she let herself in. She went round, switching on every light, as if to shut out the frightening darkness. Mrs. White wouldn't be in tonight. She had gone back to London today to see her husband. There was talk of his going to a convalescent home. The old safe life had vanished.

Never to return? Mary asked herself.

Not unless she could believe Garth, not unless she could feel that he was telling the truth.

The quietness of the house was threatening. It seemed to loom over her, like the storm clouds outside. This would be her life. Alone. Unloved. Vulnerable.

Yet she couldn't pretend to believe Garth!

Hastily she locked the door and ran down the lane to Edith.

"I'm sorry I lost my temper ... " Mary said breathlessly as she went into the long room.

Edith was stretched out on the couch, her head propped up by pillows, her red hair done up in curlers, her face covered with grease.

"Come in ... come in. I'm giving myself a beauty session," Edith said gaily. "Not that it helps much but it lifts my morale. Where've you been?"

Mary closed the door and curled up in the armchair. "I've been to Battle and

Hastings. Looking back in the past."

"And?"

"Edith, you were right. It was a narrow life," Mary said. "I never realised it before. They loved me too much . . . "

"No. They just didn't love you the right way . . . " Edith was painting her nails. Now she waved her hands about to dry the varnish. "When you really love a person, you want them to be happy. No one can find happiness unless they are taught to stand on their own feet and think for themselves."

"I agree but where do we go from there?"

Edith looked startled. "I've told you. Take a holiday. Garth'll understand. He'll close the house — I can pop in to keep an eye on things. Then he'll have the children here for Christmas and we can get that nice little Nancy Soare along to help and Mrs. White . . . "

"And a good time will be had by all," Mary said bitterly, "having got me nicely out of the way."

"For your own good, darling." Edith seized the small bottle of varnish and began to give her nails a second coat.

"Give you a chance to see the world, be a person. D'you realise, you've never lived? Just been a cabbage? A robot? You've never thought for yourself, never made a decision until now, which is why I can see some hope for your salvation . . . " Her voice was almost gay as she smiled at Mary. "Be reborn. That's what I mean. Why not go for a cruise to Africa? You'll meet strangers, learn to cope, perhaps fall in love . . . " She laughed. "Don't look so horrified. It'd do you all the good in the world. Have fun. Live. Mary, you're still young. But listen to a word of advice . . . "

She jumped up, putting the small bottle down on the table between them. "Like a drink?" Edith went barefoot across the room, her black satin trews showing her slender ankles, her painted toes.

"Mary, do me a favour," Edith went on. "Take a look in the mirror . . . It's enough to make you weep. You look nearer fifty-five than thirty-nine. Go to London to the best hairdresser and put yourself in his hands. Then have a beauty treatment and take their advice. Then go

to Harrods or Liberty — you can afford
it — and buy exciting clothes. Clothes for
the young. You're still young and could
be very attractive."

She stood above Mary, glass in hand.

"Mary, I've said some pretty beastly
things to you but I really want to help
you."

"I believe you, Edith. You're my only
real friend, the only person I can trust.
You honestly think it would help matters
if I did that? I mean, buy new clothes
and . . . and go gay? See the world
and . . ."

Edith's face was grave. "I honestly do,
Mary. I think it's the only solution."

Part Two

Garth

THE letter from Mr. Angel came as a shock to Garth. It was forwarded to him by Max, who had added a brief comment. Sitting in his office, Garth stared down at the neatly-typed letter and read it for the third time.

"I have managed to persuade Mary, who seemed very distraught, that it would be a mistake to act impulsively. I made her see that a six months' separation would be advisable. I feel that, with patience and discreet diplomacy, this matter may be settled in a satisfactory manner. I advised her not to contact you personally but to allow myself and your solicitor to handle everything."

A six months' separation! Garth whistled silently. It looked as if Mary really meant business.

He picked up Max's scribbled note. "Take everything the old boy says with a pinch of salt, Garth. All Mary wanted was someone to tell her what to do. I did — but she didn't like what I suggested. Maybe she liked the old boy's suggestion better! I'm sure Mary doesn't want a divorce any more than you do. You've got the kids to consider, for one thing; for another, what on earth would Mary do without a man to look after her! Seriously, I don't think Mary knows *what* she wants. Like all women, she's being 'ornery.' Now maybe you'll appreciate why I'm still a bachelor!"

Garth screwed up the piece of paper and tossed it in the waste paper basket. He went to the window. It was a grey chilly day, a reminder that Autumn was here.

What on earth would Mary do with herself for six months? he wondered. Was she planning to stay at the house and forbid him entrance? And what about the kids and Christmas? Three months away!

Well, he'd have to go down to Little Common and see to things. It would never occur to Mary to arrange redirection of mail, for instance. Then the house. No good closing it for several months. Better to employ Mrs. White still and ask her to keep it clean and warm. Then he'd have a good talk with Max . . .

And Edith?

He began to prowl up and down the room, hands behind his back. He hadn't much time for Edith, though the kids seemed to love her. Odd, that. Somehow you wouldn't have expected a woman like Edith liking kids. Even Voi liked her. Which was something. Which reminded him!

He hastily wrote a note to Voi, saying he hoped all was well, and what about having dinner together some time soon?

His phone bell rang. Someone to see him!

"Show him in . . . " Garth scowled. He'd never felt less like seeing anyone than at this moment but it had to be.

Posting the letter to Voi on his way back to the hotel he realised that he was not particularly happy there! His room was small though he did have a private bathroom, and the food was bearable. But he was beginning to dislike the long evenings at the office, working hard, then strolling back to the impersonal hotel, eating, having a few drinks and then to bed. Was this the way for a man to live? he wondered. And was this to go on for six months more?

Next day he rang Max. "Has Mary left the house?" Garth asked curtly, doodling on the clean blotting pad before him. "Well, find out, will you? I've got to come down to arrange things but I don't want to throw a spanner in the works." He laughed without amusement. "I'm afraid I don't thrive on melodramatic scenes."

"Sure I'll let you know, Garth," Max's voice replied. "I'll go out myself, purely official, you know . . . " He chuckled. "I might take a look at our friend, Mrs. Burrows. She fascinates me, you know."

"Edith? Fascinates you? Are you out of your mind?" Garth asked.

"You're like all people, Garth, judge by appearances. Edith's an enigma and I adore enigmas." Max laughed. "Know something? She looks so easy but she's not."

"I wouldn't have said that . . . " Garth

began and stopped.

Max was laughing. "Ah, but how far did you go, my friend? So far — and no farther, is Edith's dictum. She likes to feel she's a *femme fatale* but deep down inside her, she's a Puritan."

"You surprise me . . . " Garth began.

"I'll ring you," Max replied and rang off.

The next day, Garth got three letters. One from each child. He read Voi's first. Not because she was his favourite — sometimes, he wondered if he had a favourite. He loved each child in a different way and for totally different reasons.

Voi's letter was curt. She said she thought it an excellent idea that Mum was going away for six months. "Maybe she's anaemic or something, Dad, and this will do her good. I'm only sorry about Christmas."

Garth opened Suzy's letter next. "I didn't know Mummy was ill, did you, Daddy? I am so sorry. I wished I'd known for I would have nursed her. She seemed all rite last hols . . . " He smiled as he noted the spelling error. "Daddy, there isn't anything badly wrong with her, is there? I mean, she hasn't got t.b. or anything? Only the doctor did advise six months in sunshine and that made me think. Is she going to a sanatorium, do you think? If so, couldn't we go and see her at Christmas?"

"T.B.? Sanatorium?" Garth stared at the letter. Trust Suzy to imagine the worst. But could it be true? Had a doctor advised the six months in the sunshine? Apparently Mary had told Suzy so.

On an impulse he put a call through to Little Common. The bell rang for a long time and he was about to give up hope, when he heard Mrs. White's breathless voice.

"Sorry, Mr. Herron. I was up in the attics, tidying up."

"Is my wife there, Mrs. White?"

"No, Mr. Herron. Didn't you know, sir? She's gone to London. I helped her pack, though I must say she didn't take much and we've been making a great pile of her clothes to go to the Salvation Army. She said she was tired of most of them, and I must say they were a bit old-fashioned, if you don't mind me saying so, Mr. Herron."

"So she didn't take many clothes?" He couldn't keep the note of anxiety from his voice.

"No, Mr. Herron. She said she'd be buying more in London. I thought she was going to stay with you, Mr. Herron, and I was wondering if you was thinking of selling the house?" Now, she sounded worried, too, Garth thought.

"Certainly not, Mrs. White. Apparently . . . what I meant to say was, the doctor has been consulted and has advised Mrs. Herron to spend the next six months in the sunshine . . . "

"Oh, yes, she did say something about sunshine but I thought she was just joking. It's getting nippy down here already."

"Is she . . . " Garth paused. His hand was clenched so tightly round the receiver that he wondered if he could undo it. He moistened his dry mouth. "Is she . . . is she all right, Mrs. White?"

"All right, Mr. Herron? I think so. She seemed all right. Full of energy, too. Asked me to give the whole house a thorough spring clean. I brought my old man home the day before yesterday so it suits me very well. There's a lot of work to do, you know, Mr. Herron. It's a very big house."

"I know. Well, thanks, Mrs. White. I'll be down in a few days and we can make arrangements, then. Okay?"

"Yes, thank you, Mr. Herron, thank you very much . . . " Mrs. White was still saying as he replaced the receiver.

Garth walked to the window. And now, so what? he asked himself. The mystery deepened. Mary, full of energy, throwing away her old clothes, planning to buy new, going for six months to live in sunshine? It just didn't add up.

He said as much to Max three days later, having driven down to Bexhill.

Max's office was bright and cheerful, a modern background for Max with his black pointed beard and long hair, dark ardent eyes, one-sided grin and his rather dramatic flowing grey silk tie, and dark, Italian silk suit.

"Course it doesn't add up," Max said scornfully and tossed a packet of cigarettes across his enormous polished

112

desk. "When will anything a woman does add up? I went out to see Edith Burrows." He shrugged. "I might have been talking to a blank wall. I could get nothing out of her."

"Nothing at all?" Garth joked.

He was startled at the flash of anger on Max's face.

"Nothing at all. I told you, Garth, you're way out in your understanding of that woman. I tried to get her to explain Mary's behaviour. She said something crazy about Mary going through an adolescent stage of development and then she burst out laughing and made me feel I'd made a fool of myself."

"Did she mention Mary's health? I mean, why did the doctor advise six months in the sunshine?"

"The doctor? I think you're wrong, my friend. I gathered from the scraps of information Edith graciously gave me that it was old man Angel who suggested six months' holiday and Edith who suggested sunshine."

"She told the children the doctor advised . . . " Garth was conscious of a sense of relief, followed by anger with

Mary for having got him so worried and all for nothing.

"Oh, yes, she went to the doctor all right," Max said. "It sccms you told hcr to go and, as you know, our little Mary does what she's told. Simply because it saves her having to make decisions. Know something, Garth? She stood just over there and asked *me* what *she* should do about *you*."

Garth's cheeks felt hot. "And what did you say?"

"I told her to apologise to you and forget the whole matter."

"And what did she say?"

Max laughed, tugging at his beard. "She looked at me as if I was mad."

"I can't understand her," Garth said. "I just can't. I thought I knew Mary inside out but she's really got me stymied. Her latest is to go off to sit in the sunshine for six months, giving away her old clothes, planning to buy new. Know something, Max? She hasn't one iota of dress sense. Just not interested. Voi and I have to bully her to buy anything new. And yet, now . . . "

Max's face was suddenly grave. "There

is another angle, Garth. Personally I think it unlikely but maybe, we should consider it. Could Mary be in love with another man?"

Garth was startled by the fury that swept through him. It left him breathless, clenching his fists, filled with the impulse to hit Max for daring to suggest it.

"Of course not . . . " Garth began indignantly. And then stopped. "At least, I don't think so. But then, perhaps, I don't know . . . "

Max stood up. "I hate to throw you out, Garth, but I've a couple of appointments. I take it you're spending a night here?"

"I don't know . . . The thought of that empty house!" Garth began and then remembered Carol. It was a long time since they'd had a chat together. Not since Mary had called him a liar to his face. "Maybe I will . . . "

Max gave a funny grin. "Well, I'll be home tonight if you want company. See you."

Garth drove along the front and glanced up at Carol's flat. He'd go to the station that night, he decided, to meet her train, drive her home and they could have a friendly chat. Carol must he wondering what it was all about.

Mrs. White was painstakingly washing all the white paint in the bedrooms. Garth soon came to an arrangement with her whereby she would open up the house every day, keep an eye on the pipes and if it got very cold, she had orders to turn on the c.h. He paid her in advance.

"We'll all be here for Christmas," he said firmly.

Then he walked down the lane towards Edith Burrows'. He found her in her studio-cum-everything-else. She was painting.

"Why, Garth . . . " She looked startled.

How thin she was, he thought, her loose smock making it more obvious than usual. Even her face seemed more gaunt with the make-up she used and her bright unnaturally-red hair. He explained why he was down.

"I told Mary I'd keep an eye on the house and on Mrs. White," Edith said. "And I can always ring you, Garth, in

116

times of emergency."

Garth felt awkward, standing and staring at her. He wondered why she didn't ask him to sit down.

"Is Mary all right?" he asked.

Edith fluttered her hands. "Will she ever be all right?" she asked.

He frowned. "Look, is there anything physically wrong with Mary? I have a right to know . . ."

Unexpectedly Edith smiled. "Sit down, Garth, and I'll get us a drink. I had your friend, Max, out here, interrogating me like the F.B.I. so I'm a bit wary but I'll answer any questions, within reason."

She brought two brandies.

"First, you ask: is Mary physically well? As far as I know, she's fit as a flea, Garth."

"Did she go to the doctor?"

"You told her to go. For her migraines."

"Yes, I forgot I had! But did he order six months of sunshine?"

Edith sipped her brandy. "Not exactly. I gather he's known her for years and knowing Mary, you'll know that she wept on his shoulders and asked his advice. He thought Mr. Angel's advice of six months to think rationally about the situation was an excellent one. He thought my suggestion of a cruise to South Africa . . . "

"South Africa? Why South Africa?"

Edith shrugged. "Just that it's a pleasant cruise and a lovely country. Mary can afford that sort of holiday and I think it'll do her the world of good. The doctor agreed with me. An entirely new way of living, meeting strangers, learning to adjust and adapt herself. Something she's never had to do, Garth."

"I know. She's been too protected."

"Don't sound so apologetic, Garth. She wanted to be protected."

"But you don't want her to be?"

"No. I want her to grow up. To be a person. An individual. Not just a man's shadow. First her father's, then yours . . . What sort of life is that? She must learn to stand on her own feet."

"And you think this . . . this holiday will help her do so?"

Edith stared at him. "I sincerely hope so," she said quietly. "Garth, Mary accuses us all of being on your side and against her. She can't see how unreasonable she's being . . . "

His face showed surprise. "You mean — *you* believe me?"

"Of course," Edith said. "It could happen to anyone. After all, if every time a married man talks to a girl other than his wife, he's going to be accused of being unfaithful, well . . . what sort of life is that? There's got to be trust and . . . "

"She doesn't trust me."

"It's not that." Edith got up and refilled their glasses "Garth, believe me, she *wants* to believe you, but she can't. She describes it as a 'feeling'. A feeling she hates and fears and doesn't understand." Edith gave him back his glass.

"Garth, try and be patient. Give her a chance to find herself."

"It's just . . . "

"You've got the children to think of, Garth."

"I know, but . . . Anyhow, Mary's all right? Know where she is at this moment and when she sails?"

Edith smiled. "Yes — but don't you think it's better if you don't know?"

"Perhaps. Anyhow, Edith, you'll keep in touch? If anything happens . . . "

"Of course."

It was later when he was leaving, having politely refused her invitation to stay for a pot-luck meal, that he found himself asking: "Edith, is there another man in Mary's life?"

She looked startled. "Heavens no. What made you ask that?"

"Max . . . well, we just wondered."

She looked up at him, her lined face suddenly tired.

"Garth, I hate to say this and I hope to God I'm proved wrong, but sometimes I wonder if there is *any* man in Mary's life."

It was a sombre thought that stayed with him as he went back to the house, locked up and drove into Bexhill. Edith had put her finger on the sore spot. The one he'd ignored, been afraid to face. The truth.

Did Mary love him? Had she ever loved him at all?

Carol was not on the train. Suddenly worried, he drove down the Front to the block of flats. Carol had been at work yesterday, he was thinking, as he rang the bell.

Mrs. Walters opened the door. She looked surprised and not particularly pleased to see him.

"She's spending the night in town," she said curtly, "with a friend. I didn't know anything about it until just before she left this morning and I'd arranged to go out tonight. The young people of today are so thoughtless . . . "

Her blue-grey hair was elaborately waved, her cheeks delicately touched with rouge, her mouth cleverly made-up and he knew a moment of pity for her.

"Look, I'm on my own tonight. My wife's gone on holiday under doctor's orders. Would you like me to baby-sit?"

"That's most awfully kind of you but . . . "

"I'll go and have a quick meal and come back," he promised. "I'm fond of the boys and they know me if they wake up."

"How good of you . . . " Carol's mother said, her face bright. "I was rather disappointed, you know."

He smiled. "I know."

He had a quick dinner and went back to the flat, taking a newspaper and a paper back book he'd bought. Carol's mother was fluttering excitedly.

"I've told the boys you're here but they're good sleepers. I don't think you'll have any trouble. This is really very sweet of you, Mr. Herron . . . " She sounded as excited as a child going to her first party. "I've been so looking forward to tonight. I'll try not to be too late."

"Please don't hurry home." He went with her to the front door. "I'll be quite happy. Probably have a snooze on the couch," he told her.

He did just that. The book bored him. The quiet flat seemed impersonal. He prowled round, looking at the photos, following Carol from babyhood to womanhood, thinking what a lovely face she had. Not pretty or beautiful but there was a sort of radiance about it, a hopefulness. He wondered why she had never married again. He sprawled on the couch and slept heavily, waking only when Mrs. Walters came back.

"I'll make us a cup of chocolate . . . " she insisted. Sitting together, she told him about the wonderful evening and that she had won two prizes. Then, quite suddenly, her gaiety vanished. "Mr. Herron," she began and hesitated. "You must forgive me but . . . but is your wife really ill?"

He was puzzled and showed it, so she went on. "You know what it is like in a small town. Gossip." She shrugged. "Maybe I shouldn't listen to it but I got a bit worried the way your name was being linked with Carol's. The neighbours."

That jerked him out of sleepy drowsiness. "My name linked with Carol's?"

"I'm sorry if I offended you but . . . but I don't want Carol hurt. She's been hurt enough, already," Mrs. Walters went on firmly. "There's talk that you and your wife are separating and then . . . then someone got to saying that you and Carol were always together and . . . and I got worried."

Looking into her anxious face, he bent forward to touch her hand lightly. "I promise you that there is nothing between Carol and me except friendship, Mrs. Walters. We are not always together. When we travel on the same trains, we talk, for we work for the same firm. Wouldn't it be strange if we didn't talk? I give her lifts home so that you can go out early. Is that wrong of us?" he spoke gently but there was a firmness unmistakably in his voice. "I assure you that your daughter and I are not in love. There always is gossip but it has no foundation. My wife is not ill. She suffers from migraines and has been advised by the doctor to take a long holiday. She is going to South Africa to enjoy the sunshine. That's all."

He thought suddenly that he hoped he was telling the truth and that the situation was as simple as that!

Mrs. Walters looked relieved. "Thank you, Mr. Herron. You see, I don't know if Carol's told you but her husband's deserted her three times . . . "

"Her husband? I thought she was a widow?"

"Everyone thinks so, Mr. Herron, but she isn't. He's a bad man, I think, but Carol's so soft she always forgives him. He deserted her ten months after they were married just when she'd had the twins. Four years later, he turned up and moved in. He stayed with her six months and left her . . . well, about to have a child. The child was still-born. Three years later, back he comes, and that soft-hearted girl forgives him and they start again. He lasts out a year this time. Their baby was a month old when it caught polio and he walked out again. The baby died." She paused and Garth said nothing. What was there to say? He was filled with overwhelming pity for Carol.

"I keep telling her to divorce him. But it isn't as easy as that for he just vanishes. Besides I don't think she would. She thinks he needs her . . . " the old lady snorted. "And how he needs her!" she said. "Just to make use of her when it suits him. She's having a hard battle bringing up the two boys and helping me out. She's a fine girl and I'm proud of her and I don't want her to get hurt."

Garth stood up. "Thanks for confiding in me, Mrs. Walters. I understand how you feel. Well, I can safely promise you that I will never hurt Carol — intentionally. We rarely see one another these days. I honestly don't think you need worry," he said.

Driving home through the cold night with a mist floating along Barnhorn Road, he wondered if he was right. He hoped he was. Carol was too nice a person to be allowed to get involved with a married man.

How unpleasant that sounded, he thought, as the two Alsatians in the house next door, barked as he drove in.

"Involved with a married man," he repeated. How dirty it sounded!

A few days later, Garth had a phone call that worried him. It was from the Matron at the Hostel, where Voi lived.

"I'd be grateful, Mr. Herron, if you'd have a talk with Voi. She's being rather troublesome these days."

"Voi? Troublesome?"

He must have sounded indignant for her voice was apologetic.

"I know it sounds absurd for she's such a good girl but lately ... well, Mr. Herron, she will not respect the rules. She comes home at night late. She doesn't tell us when she's going to be out to dinner. She's been missing some of the lectures, I understand. I know this is not a school for children but a college for young adults. All the same, we must have certain rules and see that they're obeyed."

"Quite! I'll see Voi."

"Please, Mr. Herron, keep silent about this. I don't want Voi to feel she is being persecuted. She's suffering from a heavy attack of self-pity at the moment, Mr. Herron."

He was startled. "She is?"

"Didn't you know, Mr. Herron?" the Matron asked gently. "What a pity." And Garth caught his breath. He knew what she meant. That, as one of Voi's parents, he should have known that something had happened to hurt Voi very much indeed.

"Yes, it is," he said quietly. "I'll ring her tonight and make an arrangement to meet her. Thank you very much for calling me."

He put down the phone and sat back in his chair, sighing. What had happened to his quiet life? he wondered. Everything had changed. And not for the better. It was as if the pattern of his life had been cut up into small pieces and tossed in a waste paper basket. How would he put the pieces together? he wondered. If he ever could!

★ ★ ★

Dinner with Voi proved surprisingly difficult to arrange as she seemed to have so many 'dates' so, in the end, he had to get rather parental and insist on having some of her time.

"All right, Dad," she sounded resigned. "I'll cancel tomorrow's date and I'll meet you — where?"

"Rainbow Restaurant," he said. He wondered if he should ask Bob, too, but decided not to. He must find some way to talk to Voi. There must be a way. He'd always managed to in the past.

But the past was the past and the present was not so easy, he found, the next day. The hesitation showing on her face and the restrained way she kissed him told him that he had a difficult job ahead of him.

She had changed! Her long fair hair looked grubby and unkempt, as if she hadn't combed it for months. Her make-up was so excessive as to make her face a caricature with slanting eyes, ridiculous lashes, far too much lipstick. Her dress was a gay crimson under a black cape which was lined with candy-striped silk. Her voice was loud, her eyes too bright as if there were tears near.

"Your mother's going to South Africa," Garth said after he'd ordered the dinner.

"Is she." Voi sounded disinterested. "For ever?"

He was shocked. "Of course not. Just for six months. It'll do her good. The sunshine, meeting people . . . "

"It sounds revolting."

"My dear Voi . . . "

"I am not your dear Voi . . . " she suddenly said, her voice too loud for his comfort and he glanced round uneasily. Luckily, no one seemed to have noticed. "I am sick and tired of this hypo . . . hypocritical charm you turn on. You are being pompous, a prig and . . . " her voice broke and she stopped speaking.

Then she looked up and met his startled gaze. "Sorry, Dad. I didn't mean to let fly. It's just that . . . "

"That?"

She shrugged. "Just — that!"

The Chicken 'a la King arrived and there was no need to talk. Later Garth sought the right words but couldn't find any. Desperately he enquired politely of Bob.

"A nice lad, Voi. Is he all right?"

It was the wrong thing to say. He knew it as soon as he had said the words. Her face went furiously red, her eyes blazed.

"Bob! All right! He walked out on me. And I don't blame him."

"He . . . walked out on you? I don't get it."

She glared. "Don't you? Don't pretend, Dad. You and Mum got rid of him all right. I don't blame him. That . . . that awful . . . awful aura of anger. Every time Mum spoke, you felt it. Then you and Mum . . . all that about preferring Bexhill station . . . I wanted to be sick. Just sick . . . " Her voice faltered. "Well, he got scared, I guess, and just ran."

He drew a deep breath.

"Voi, there must be a reason. Bob isn't the sort of man to act like that."

"Isn't he?" she said bitterly. "Then

130

why haven't I heard from him?"

"There must be a reason," Garth repeated. "If . . . if you really cared for Bob, you'd trust him."

"You men are all the same . . . " Voi told him, her voice still unsteady and a little thick. "You think you can do just what you like and we must 'trust' you. Trust! He could at least have phoned me, or . . . or sent me a card."

Garth saw the pain on her face and he ached with helplessness. Poor darling. If he could only help . . . This, then, was why Voi was being 'troublesome'. Because of her feeling of being rejected, she had to prove that Bob meant nothing to her, so she was probably going out with the wrong type of boys just to 'show' Bob. A sudden fear split through Garth as he stared at her young unhappy face.

"Voi, give him a little time. He seemed such a decent lad. We had quite a long talk on the way to the station. He definitely gave me the impression that he was quite smitten." Garth smiled at her. "Darling, maybe he's ill. There's sure to be a reason. You shouldn't jump to conclusions."

He put his hand on hers but she jerked hers free and glared at him. "It's easy for you to talk. You just don't understand."

The whole evening was the same. Unprofitable and worrying. He could not get through her defiant defence. Everything he said was wrong. He took her to a good film and heard her quietly sniffling all through it. But when he tried to comfort her, she snapped at him. Finally, it was with relief that he delivered her to the Hostel in good time, for it had been a tiring and miserable evening. He had achieved nothing. Nor had he helped poor Voi, at all. That evening in his miserable hotel room, he faced facts. This was no way to live. If Mary was going to be away for six months, he could choose either to commute to Little Common daily and let Mrs. White look after him, or else rent a furnished flat and eat all his meals out. But he needed something better than a hotel room.

He made the decision but that was all, for the days dragged by and he seemed unable to do anything about it. Was it, he wondered, because subconsciously he hoped Mary would change her mind, perhaps phone him, and they could start again?

Yet remembering her fury, her shrill voice, he shivered. He just couldn't stand that sort of scene again.

One wet October day he stood by the window gazing down at the rain-swept streets, the wretched people scurrying along under umbrellas that threatened to collide, the huge red buses swerving round corners at what looked like perilous angles, the perpetual moving stream of cars and he thought he'd never felt so miserable before. Maybe it would do *him* good to take a six months' holiday and go and sit in the sun!

He smiled wryly at the thought of the other partners' faces if he dared suggest such a thing. Besides, what on earth would he do with himself, just sitting in the sunshine? He'd be bored to tears at the end of three weeks!

The door opened and he swung round. Ella, the new young receptionist, stood there, her long fair hair reaching to her shoulders, her plump little face worried.

"Mr. Herron, I don't know what to do," she began anxiously. "There's a lady who wants to see one of the advisers. I don't know who to send her to. She says she's never been here before . . . "

"What's she like, Ella? Young, old, middle-aged? Rich, poor, eccentric?"

Ella smiled. "Well, she's not young. In her thirties, I'd say. But she must be rich. She's got an absolutely super-duper fur coat on. Could be mink. And a very elegant Cossack fur hat. Oh, and she must be eccentric for she's wearing dark glasses."

Garth laughed. It was a pleasant change, he thought, to find something to laugh at!

"I'll come along and see her and probably introduce her to young Petrie."

"Thanks, Mr. Herron . . . " Ella looked relieved and Garth stood up to follow her. She almost ran and Garth said loudly, "Tell her I'll be right along."

At the end of the corridor where it turned to the reception hall, a door opened and Carol came out.

"Oh, Mr. Herron . . . " She was looking upset. "Could I have a word?"

"Of course. Tell our client I'll be with her in two minutes, Ella," Garth said loudly and turned to look down at Carol.

Her face was white.

"I must talk to you . . . " she said earnestly.

He was puzzled. It wasn't like Carol to talk to him here at the office if she could avoid it.

"Of course. Could you stay up tomorrow and we'll have dinner together? I saw your mother . . . "

"I know . . . it was only last night that she told me she'd had a talk with you . . . "

Carol sounded so miserable that without thought, Garth put his hand on her arm.

"Look, Carol, ring your mother you'll be late and we'll have dinner together tonight . . . Okay?"

Some of the unhappiness left her face.

"Thanks, Garth . . . " she said very softly.

He smiled and turned to hurry to the reception hall, just in time to see the flick of a fur coat as the woman, waiting to see him, got into the lift and the door slid to.

The lift had gone by the time he reached the reception desk. Ella was looking puzzled. "She didn't say anything, Mr. Herron. I told her you'd only be a minute and she just stared across at you and . . . and just then someone got out of the lift and she just . . . well, she just ran and got into it . . ."

"Perhaps I look formidable and scared her . . . " Garth joked. But he was puzzled and as he walked back to his office, found himself wondering who the devil it could have been. She couldn't have blamed him for keeping her waiting for he'd talked to Carol for barely a few seconds. Maybe she'd changed her mind and decided to keep her money safe in the bank, rather than invest it in shares, he told himself. But the memory of the young woman in a fur coat, a fur hat, and sunglasses on a wet day, stayed with him.

He'd been in his office barely five minutes when Stuart Kendall sent for him. A little curious, Garth went.

Stuart Kendall was a man in his late sixties. One of the older partners, he was the one with most influence in the firm. He was also the one Garth liked and respected and viewed his future retirement with dismay. Stuart had a happy knack of handling people, making them do what he wanted but firmly believing that it was what they wanted to do.

Now he stood at the window. A massive man with broad shoulders, snow-white hair and an Imperial beard.

"A miserable day! Sit down, Garth, my boy. How are things?"

He turned to look at Garth. His skin was pocked with small brown freckles, his thick-rimmed glasses slid down his beak-like nose.

Garth was surprised. "Why, I'm fine, thanks."

"And your wife?"

The timbre of Stuart's voice had changed and Garth stiffened. So that was what Stuart wanted to see him about!

"She's fine, too."

"I gather she's away . . . ?"

"She's going to South Africa for six months."

"South Africa? Have you relations there?" Stuart sounded interested.

Garth smiled. "No. And I haven't a clue as to why she chose South Africa, Stuart, and that's the truth."

"Why's she going?"

Garth stood up and joined his companion at the window, down which trickled rain. "I don't honestly know, Stuart. This summer we had a . . . well, a few words. She accused me of something and when I told the truth, she refused to believe me. Things got worse and . . . well, they've never got better."

"Are you getting a divorce?" Stuart's voice was dismayed. He believed in happy marriages and that his colleagues should have secure backgrounds.

"I sincerely hope not," Garth said. "And my solicitor and hers . . . "

"It's got as far as that?" Stuart sounded shocked.

"Well, yes and no. It's hard to explain what has happened," Garth said, sticking his hands in his pockets and wishing the conversation could end. "We had a few words, as I said, and we've been living apart. Mary won't believe me and I refuse to confess to something I didn't do."

"Is that what she wants?"

Garth shrugged. "Goodness knows. She doesn't seem to know herself. She'd been having migraines and saw a doctor. Apparently he thought it'd be a good idea for her to get right away. Anyhow, she's gone for six months and I gather, from what my solicitor and hers said, that when she comes back the situation will be reviewed . . . " He finished bitterly: "It's not very pleasant being called a liar by your wife."

"My dear fellow, I'm sure it isn't," Stuart said soothingly. "You were telling her the truth?"

Garth's eyes flashed. "I most certainly was."

Stuart smiled. "I'm sure you were, but lots of husbands lie to their wives for the sake of peace."

"Well, I'm not going to lie about this and pretend to be sorry I did something that I didn't do . . . "

"A most delightful sentence, my dear

boy." Stuart laughed. "Come and sit down. I've a very disagreeable task to do and I think a drink is indicated."

Garth obeyed, feeling a cold tremor shoot through him. What could be the 'disagreeable task' Stuart dreaded doing?

Over the drinks he learned. Stuart had heard that Carol Stirn and Garth Herron had been seen together several times and there was gossip that this alliance was the cause of Garth's wrecked marriage.

"But blast it . . . " Garth exploded, "my marriage is not wrecked nor have I an alliance with Carol Stirn."

Stuart smiled apologetically. "I'm sure you haven't, my dear fellow, but people are talking."

"But . . . " Garth swallowed and tried to control his temper. "Look, Stuart . . . " he leaned forward over the mahogany desk. "Carol and I travel on the same trains to and from Bexhill. We've got into the habit of travelling together. I know her mother well, and her twin sons. Indeed, I have done some baby-sitting for the old lady. I have, on occasion, gone to their flat for a drink. I am not having an alliance with Carol Stirn nor is she with me . . . In any case, she's married . . . "

A slight smile played round Stuart's mouth. "Does that necessarily make any difference? I thought she was a widow."

"So did I . . . " Garth said and stopped abruptly. He saw amusement in Stuart's eyes and felt a fool.

"Look, Stuart, I give you my word that there is nothing at all between Carol and myself. Why, I haven't seen her, except occasionally in the office, since my wife and . . . "

"Was it about Carol that you and your wife disagreed?" Garth sighed. "Look, it was and it wasn't. It's just so childish I . . . I could . . . " He bit his mouth and looked down at Stuart.

"Look, I've commuted from Little Common for twenty years. I always went from Cooden. Then I decided to go from Bexhill. I told my wife but she didn't remember. She's often vague about things like that. Then last summer, she found out by chance that I was travelling to and from Bexhill and accused me of not telling her. Then she . . . " Garth strode to the window. This was the part that hurt.

"She followed me or rather, she waited one evening for me to arrive. She saw me with Mrs. Stirn, followed my car and saw me drive Carol . . . Mrs. Stirn home."

"Which, I gather, you did every night?"

"Yes. Was that a crime? Anyhow, Mary refused to believe me. Called me a liar and so . . . "

"You left home?" Stuart followed him to the window. "A crazy story, my dear fellow, so crazy that I believe you."

Garth swung round, his face relieved. "Thanks . . . "

The older man lifted his hand. "Unfortunately it does not alter the situation. As you are well aware, it was your father who made it plain that he would not allow business and pleasure to mix in the office. It was his rule that when any couple became enamoured of one another, married or engaged, one of the couple must leave . . . " He paused and looked at Garth.

"We are proud of our name, Garth. The matter has been discussed and we are disturbed by the gossip already moving round. I'm afraid Mrs. Stirn must go."

Garth caught his breath and then lost his temper.

"That's most unfair. She needs the job. Her husband's deserted her three times and she has to partly support her mother and fully support the twins. She needs the job . . . "

Stuart nodded. "And we need her. She is an extremely efficient young woman. She will have no difficulty in obtaining another job. I will see personally to that, Garth."

"But it's so unfair. She . . . we . . . we've done nothing wrong. A friendly chat on the train . . . "

"My dear boy, I believe you, but who would? A friendly chat on the train can lead to stronger emotions. The way you leapt to her defence, your knowledge of her financial status proves that you are good friends. That could be the start, Garth. Your wife going off for six months was a grave error on her part. She's practically thrown you into the young woman's arms."

"I haven't seen her . . . "

"You were seen talking to her today.

I gather Mrs. Stirn was distressed about something?"

"Why, that's only a few moments ago . . . " Garth's temper rose rapidly. "Am I being watched? Followed . . . "

Stuart smiled. "Calm down, Garth. Of course not. We've already discussed the matter. I stated firmly that I felt certain that you knew what you were doing and that you and Mrs. Stirn were not close friends. Unfortunately a certain rather malicious person in the firm — no names, naturally, saw you and Mrs. Stirn talking, saw also that you lost a client through your delayed interview with her — all this because you paused to talk to Mrs. Stirn, so I was told. She also heard you arrange to meet Mrs. Stirn for dinner. I was immediately informed and therefore sent for you, Garth. This can't be allowed to go on. I know it sounds Victorian, that you have every right to say that you are free to lead your own life, but I must remind you that it has always been the policy of the firm to allow no scandal, no close friendships between members of the staff." He stood up. "Mrs. Stirn must go. I will see that

144

she is not harmed financially, Garth, and that she gets as good, if not better, a job than this one. I'm sorry but that's the way it is."

Garth stared at him. His first impulse was to hand in his resignation, say that he would sell his partnership in the firm and clear out. But commonsense stopped him. He drew a long deep breath.

"I'm sorry, Stuart. I think you're making a grave mistake and being extremely unjust to both Mrs. Stirn and myself." He walked with dignity to the door and turned. "Don't tell her until tomorrow, Stuart. I'll break the news tonight. I'm afraid she's going to be very upset," he added as he closed the door.

★ ★ ★

His words proved right, Garth found, later that evening but not quite as he had expected. He had taken Carol to a quiet restaurant with a long corridor which had small alcoves where, though the guests could be seen, there was a certain amount of privacy and you were sufficiently far enough away from your neighbours to be able to talk in peace. The lights were dim, there was soft music, good food, but from the beginning of the evening, Carol was tense.

She waited until the waiter had left them.

"Garth, I'm terribly sorry . . . " she began, the words tumbling out. "I didn't realise Mother had talked to you like that. I'm so sorry . . . I feel dreadful . . . "

"Your mother talked to me like what? I don't get it," Garth asked.

Carol looked down at her hands. She was wearing a lime green woollen frock with a matching coat. Her face was unhappy. She looked so different from the Carol of a few months back, he thought.

"Talking about Don — that's my husband and . . . and us." Garth saw that Carol's cheeks were red. "I was so embarrassed, Garth. And upset. Mother had no right . . . "

He put his hand over hers. "She has a right, Carol. The right of love. She was afraid you'd get hurt again. I explained our friendship and that it was nothing more . . . "

She began to speak but the wine waiter was there, showing Garth the bottle, opening it, pouring a little in his glass, standing back in the usual ritual of wine tasting until Garth nodded approvingly.

When he had gone, Garth smiled at her. "Honestly, Carol, sometimes I think I am going mad. I feel a bit like Alice must have felt when she stepped through the looking glass. Everything has changed. Nothing is the same."

Carol managed a smile. "Nothing's the same," she agreed.

"I just can't understand how it all happened," Garth ran his hand through his thick dark hair. "Sometimes I want to scream. Sometimes I think this must be a nightmare, and one day I'll wake up. I only wish I could."

"You do? You're not happy?" Carol's voice was low.

"Happy? I'll say I'm not. Life's an absolute mess at the moment. My wife's gone off to South Africa for six months . . . my daughter's broken her heart, I'm living in a miserable bedroom of a lousy hotel and now . . . "

He sighed. "Carol, this isn't going to be easy, Kendall hauled me over the coals this afternoon. Seems there's gossip in the office about us."

"About us?" Carol stared at him. "About us?"

"I know. It's crazy, isn't it. What have we done? Sat in the same train and talked. You've invited me to meet your mother and the twins. Maybe I've had a drink or two with you. And out of that, they've managed to make some gossip. Apparently someone heard us this afternoon and Kendall was told that you were very distressed and that I arranged to take you out to dinner . . . "

Carol stared at him. "But . . . "

"That's how I feel. Kendall was very upset and apologetic. There's a ruling in the firm, perhaps you've heard of it. It's as extinct as the dodo and was instituted by my dear father, who was a Victorian in the wrong era and insisted that business and pleasure must never be mixed and no two members of the staff are allowed to marry, be engaged or become close friends." He stared at her startled face. "I don't know how to tell you, Carol, but you must leave the firm."

"Lose my job . . . ?" Carol's voice rose in dismay. "But I need it."

Garth covered her hand with his. "I know. I explained all that, Kendall says he'll see that you get as good, if not better, a job and he'll see, also, that you do not suffer financially. Oh, Carol, I'm sorry to have done this to you . . . "

She smiled. It was a moving, poignant smile. Weak. Her eyes moist as if with tears unshed. But somehow she had found the courage to smile.

"It's not your fault, Garth."

"I'm afraid it is. I should have foreseen what would happen. I'm terribly sorry, Carol. I told your mother I would never hurt you — intentionally."

"And you haven't, Garth," Carol said quickly. "Don't blame yourself." She held his hand against her cheek. "I don't really mind about the job. I'll get another. And it'll be easier for us, Garth. To meet, I mean. We can have lunch together . . . we'll find a way."

He looked at her. Her cheeks were

flushed, her eyes shining. Now she was kissing his hand.

"Carol . . . I don't want you to get hurt," he said quickly, trying to free his hand but she clung to it. "You mustn't get involved with me . . . "

"Oh, Garth, it's too late. I am in love with you. I've loved you for ages. I know it's hopeless but . . . "

Voi

NEXT day, Voi phoned her father to apologise.

"I really am sorry, Dad," she said. "You gave me a wonderful evening and I was an absolute swine. I'd no right to take it out on you for it isn't your fault . . ."

He sighed. "I don't think it's easy to say whose fault it is, darling. Anyhow, thanks for ringing me. I quite understand how you feel, even though you think I don't. By the way, I've decided to take a furnished flat. In fact I'm going out to see it tonight. Just off Church Street. You know, near Kensington High Street."

"Oh yes. Dad, why are you taking it?"

"Because I'm sick and tired of this hotel I'm in. I loathe the bedroom and . . . well, if your mother is going to be away for six months, I can't go on living like this."

"What about your meals? I mean, can you cook, Dad?"

"I've never tried but I guess I can learn. In any case, I'll probably eat out. Saves washing up."

They both laughed.

"I'll ring you, Voi, for we must have another evening together soon. Okay?"

"Okay, Dad."

When Voi rang off, she ran up the stairs to her room, slammed the door and made herself a cup of coffee, curling up on the divan, putting on a record. She sighed. What was it Dad had said: "I don't think it's easy to say whose fault it is."

He was being very good for it was obviously all Mum's fault. Making Dad live on his own, upsetting them all and for why? Simply because she couldn't believe something he'd said!

She sipped the hot coffee slowly. She thought that she had never been so unhappy in all her life. She could have gone out that evening but she was tired of the boys her friends went about with. They were so young. Students, most of them.

No one like Bob. Bob wasn't always talking about what he would do 'one day', he was already going ahead in his career. He was ambitious but he didn't expect success to be suddenly there. He knew he'd have to work hard and be patient. Bob had, what the Matron of the Hostel would say: 'both feet firmly on the ground'. As a rule that type of man was a bore but Bob wasn't. Bob was different! If only . . . if only she'd never suggested that weekend visit to Little Common. If only Bob hadn't accepted. If only both Mum and Dad had controlled themselves, instead of losing their tempers and letting it be so obvious.

Oldies were queer cattle. Another expression Matron was fond of using! They preached but never practised what they'd preached. Dad was forever telling them about the need to control tempers. He talked of self-discipline, ethics, right and wrong and all that, but . . .

She put the cup down on the table and buried her face in the pillow. It seemed as if she was always crying these days.

There was this terrible emptiness inside her. This bleak feeling that something wonderful had happened to her and that somehow, it had vanished. She'd lost something that meant more to her than anything else.

Next day Voi phoned her father and asked him out to dinner. He sounded quite pleased.

That'll be lovely."

Voi went to a lot of trouble, brushing her hair carefully, only lightly making-up, choosing a deep blue velveteen dress.

Her father whistled softly when he saw her and tucked her hand under his arm.

"You look good enough to eat," he said cheerfully.

Over dinner, he described his new flat.

"It's on the second floor and I have a big sitting-room, a sleeping alcove and a kitchen that's in a cupboard. I have a bathroom of my own. It's not home but it's better than that lousy hotel . . . "

"You did hate the hotel, Dad, didn't you. When are you moving?"

"Saturday. Sunday I'm going down to see Robbie. I heard from the School Matron that he's been having asthma attacks. He's never had them in the past?"

"No. Never."

Her father pulled a letter out of his pocket. "I heard from Suzy. It seems Robbie wrote to her and told her about these attacks. I think young Robbie is enjoying the fuss that's being made over them. Anyhow, she says . . . " Voi watched her father smile as he read out:

"'Asthma is usually due to a nervous condition, Dad. It's obvious to me that this is due to Mummy going away. Robbie is a child and needs her. I think you should tell her.'"

"Our Suzy knows all the answers, doesn't she, Voi? So full of long words. I can't imagine what she'll be like when she grows up."

"Either brilliant or quite impossible, Dad."

He laughed. "I think you're right, darling. Anyhow, she's concerned at my living in a hotel. Says there is a lot of food poisoning going about. I'll write and tell her I've taken a flat. That'll please her."

155

"Ought we to tell Mum about Robbie's asthma?" Voi asked.

Her father looked suddenly very tired. "I don't know her address. If it was serious, I can ask Mrs. Burrows for it, of course, but . . . Actually, I think the School Matron may be exaggerating. She is a bit of a fusser if I remember rightly. That reminds me, Voi. Can you bear to talk about Bob? Have you heard from him? I think if you really love him, you should be able to trust him."

Voi stiffened. "Dad — I don't want to talk about him. I've often wondered if — Dad, you never told me the reason you left Mum? Would you mind?"

"I left Mum? Well, I suppose in a way I did . . . " He turned his glass round slowly as he spoke. "I'll tell you the whole story." Voi listened silently, imagining her father sitting by the woman in the train, just talking, dropping her off at home, going in for a drink.

"And that was all?"

"Yes, Voi. The train journeys are long and can be boring. Mrs. Stirn is intelligent and amusing. I've grown sorry

156

for her mother and fond of her sons. But that's all."

He went on to tell her how her mother had found out.

"That's what hurt me most. The thought of her snooping."

"And she didn't believe you? I would have . . . " Voi said eagerly.

He smiled sadly. "You say that but you don't trust Bob. After all, he or someone in his family might be ill. Why not write to him? Or phone his parents . . . "

Voi frowned. "Dad . . . you never were good at lying or . . . or fooling me. What have you been up to? What do you know?"

He looked a bit ashamed. "Nothing much, darling. Just that I went down to Esher and made a few enquiries . . . "

"You — did — what?"

"Well, just asked a few questions and they said . . . "

Voi pushed her chair back so roughly that it fell over. "I don't want to know . . . how could you do this to me, Dad? How could you humiliate me? What will Bob think of me . . . " Her voice rose.

"Look, Voi, Bob's . . . "

But Voi did not wait to hear. She turned, grabbed her cape from the hook and ran out of the restaurant, down the cold dark street to the nearest bus, jumping on it, hurrying back to the sanctuary of her room, slamming and locking the door, standing in the middle of the small room, hands to her burning face. How could he do this to her. How could he! How Bob would despise her! Oh — it was terrible. If she could only die.

She saw everything very differently in the morning. Poor Dad had only been trying to help! Parents had such queer ideas but he had meant well.

And what, she wondered, had he found out about Bob? Obviously something had happened to keep Bob from writing or getting in touch with her because Dad was still on his side.

She phoned her father in the first break. A little nervously, even as she stood in the cramped public callbox, she rehearsed the words again and again. How could she ask casually what he had found out about Bob?

When it came to it, she couldn't. Her mouth was dry.

"I'm terribly sorry, Dad," she began, "for . . . for last night. I know you meant well but . . . "

"Why, Voi darling . . . " her father sounded tolerant. "You don't need to apologise. I was the one at fault. I've no right to interfere in your affairs."

"You only wanted to help me, I know, Dad."

He laughed. "It isn't easy being a parent, Voi. Whatever we do is wrong. I hate to say it, darling, but I must rush. I've an urgent appointment. 'Bye . . . "

"Bye . . . " she said but the click had gone. She put down the receiver slowly, feeling a desolate feeling of failure. Why, oh why, she asked herself, had she lacked the courage to ask him about Bob?

It was the same every time they met. Voi would spend hours beforehand planning what she would say, how casually she would lead up to it, but each time when she dined with him, something seemed to die inside her. It was as if her anger had built up an iron curtain between them. She sensed that her father was as tense as she was, just as afraid of getting on to the subject of Bob as she was eager to do so.

Sometimes she was tempted to phone Bob's parents. Perhaps he was ill, perhaps he thought she was being unfriendly in not trying to find out where he was. A dozen times she went to the callbox. She had already looked up his parents' phone number. But each time she lacked the courage. She would hear their phone bell ring and slam down the receiver. What could she say? How could she word it?

"Is Bob ill? Only he hasn't written to me . . . "

Could she ask that? And how would Bob react? Bob was not the type of man who'd like to be chased.

So the days passed and November drew near with its threats of fogs and wet winds. And still no word from Bob.

One evening, dining with her father and going back afterwards to his flat in Kensington, she told him of a letter she'd had from Suzy.

Looking round the white-walled sitting-room with its big divan covered with crimson velvet and its dozens of small cushions, and the curtained alcove where her father's bed was, Voi said:

"She's worried about you, Dad. She says man was not born to live alone . . . " She laughed suddenly. "I honestly don't know where Suzy gets these clichés."

"Lots of men live alone quite happily," her father said, carefully pouring out coffee for them both.

"That's different. Suzy guessed you'd say that, for she adds: 'When a man's been used to having a woman around, it must be pretty miserable.'" Voi put back her head, her hair swinging slightly. "Oh, Dad, isn't she the end! Anyhow to make it brief, she thinks I ought to live with you so that you've got a woman round the place . . . " she finished with a giggle.

Her father stared at her. A strange look on his face.

"Suzy thinks I . . . I should have a woman round the place," he said slowly.

"Yes. She thinks it's my duty to come and look after you, make your bed, iron your shirts, clean your shoes and cook . . . " Voi laughed again. "Oh, honestly!"

Her father didn't smile. He frowned slightly.

"I don't know how you feel about it, Voi, but maybe we should think it over." He turned away, hunting in a cupboard as if looking for something but when he turned round, there was nothing in his hand.

"It might be an idea, Voi," he said, still speaking slowly. "It would solve a lot of problems."

Those words stayed with her during the next days. She had been against the idea, pleading the long distance it was from the Commercial College, the bus rides, the wet foggy mornings when she'd have to leave so early. For some reason or other, she didn't want to keep house for her father. She wasn't sure why!

She was trying to work hard, obeying the rules of the Hostel, pretending to herself and her friends that everything was hunky-dory. Sometimes she went to the discotheques with them, or to pop shows, but she didn't enjoy them. Now they seemed noisy and childish. And deep inside her was this ache.

If only she knew where and how Bob

was. If only she'd the courage to ask her father. If only . . .

And then she had the bright idea. She had it the day before she rang her father at his flat and got a shock.

The idea came first. If her father had gone to Esher — why couldn't she? But suppose Bob saw her . . . ? Well, she'd have to think up some excuse. Was there some very old house down there, or a museum or a special kind of church? If she looked Esher up in the library, she might get a clue and go down there. Perhaps, just perhaps, she might meet someone friendly. In one of the shops? What excuse could she have? She wondered. She might go to the church to look at . . . what did you look at in old churches? Gravestones? stained-glass windows? Surely there must be something. And maybe she could mention casually that a friend of hers lived somewhere near.

She was thrilled. This might be the answer. But all this was before she phoned her father.

Then there was a new fear. Her father was out when she rang. And a female voice answered the phone.

"I'm afraid Mr. Herron'll be late home tonight. He's been delayed. Can I give a message?"

It was a pleasant, even a friendly voice.

But Voi didn't answer. She slammed down the receiver and stood, hand pressed against her mouth as she remembered.

Little incidents she'd hardly noticed at the time. Her father's hesitation when they first talked about her living with him. His complete change later when he asked her to and said strangely: "It might solve many problems."

His insistence, also, that she always phone him before she went round to his flat. "I might be out or entertaining a business friend."

A business friend! Voi thought. Oh, Daddy!

Mary

MARY lay in a deck chair on the boat deck. Her eyes half-open, she gazed up at the cloudless blue sky and at the funnel, squat and red with its black top.

It was strange, this life at sea, she thought drowsily, listening vaguely to the shouts and laughter coming from the swimming-pool.

"Time to move out of the sun, Mary ... " a deep masculine voice ordered.

She smiled as she stared at the man in the deck chair by her side. "It's so lovely."

He smiled back. A lean hungry-looking man with dark eyes and short dark hair, now he sat up.

"But you'll be mad if you get burned."

She sat up obediently. "I know ... "

"Let's go along and get us a cold drink," he suggested, helping her to her feet, holding the pale yellow towelling coat for her to slide her arms in before she fastened it round her with the gold chain belt. She glanced down at her yellow bikini and wondered what Voi would say if she could see her!

And Garth!

She slid her mind away from the name quickly and turned to smile at her companion. "Dirk, I'm literally dying of thirst."

He laughed and then tucked his hand through her arm and led the way down the deck.

The ship was rolling slightly, but on either side the great sea stretched away to distant horizons, molten silver in the sunshine, a gentle swell on the turgid water with only a few flecks of foam.

"I often wonder, Mary," he said, "how you managed to get on board this ship alone. You are such a docile biddable one, only doing what you're told."

"That's twenty years of marriage, I suppose. It's always so much easier to do what you're told than to argue about it."

"The line of least resistance," he said thoughtfully as he led her to a chair at one of the tables outside the Lido. The steward came quickly with a smile.

Mary relaxed in the comfortable chair. How very pleasant it was, she thought, still a little sleepy.

Dirk leaned forward. "Have you any idea how beautiful you are?" he said softly.

Startled, she began to laugh. No one in her life had called her that! Certainly she looked very different now from what she had done when she had led that cabbage like existence, to quote Edith's words, in Little Common.

"Of course not," she said lightly. "My parents brought me up to be modest . . ." She looked down at her clasped hands demurely and then gave him a quick smile.

He laughed. "You're wonderful, Mary. Which is the real you, I wonder. This quiet, placid little woman or the devil that glints in your eyes at times."

"Does it?" She was really surprised. Was that, she wondered, what Edith called flirting?

"Seriously, though, you'd break the heart of any artist. How to catch that look of innocence on your face, the frailty of your skin, your high cheekbones, that seductive mouth . . . ”

“Seductive?” Mary tried to laugh. His hand was over hers, holding it tightly for a moment before he let go of it.

“Yes, seductive, my darling. I wonder if you realise it is . . . ”

The steward came at that moment with the long ice-filled drinks and Mary was glad. Sometimes Dirk disturbed her with his intensity.

“What made you come on this trip alone? When I saw you, wandering, lost down in the bowels of this ship, I felt sure that there must be a husband round somewhere,” Dirk went on. Offering her a cigarette, lighting it, cupping the lighter and her hand as she put the cigarette in her mouth. “I was so thankful when you told me you’d left your husband at home. But why did he let a beauty like you travel alone?”

“Oh, Dirk,” she laughed. “You’re so corny at times. Garth and I . . . ” Her voice lost its laughter and her face clouded. “Well, we had a difference and . . . and I was advised to take a holiday for six months in the sun and . . . and think things over."

Dirk was watching her with those narrowed eyes of his.

"Thinking about divorce?"

"Oh no . . . " Mary began and stopped. "I don't know. I honestly don't know," she said, completely unaware of the wistfulness in her voice. "We've been married twenty years and then there are the children and . . . I don't know. I just don't know."

He was silent for a moment and then said: "I'm glad you chose this ship."

Mary smiled. "I didn't. My friend, Edith, got fed up with me because I couldn't seem to decide or do anything. I just drifted. So she rang the shipping people, managed to get the cancellation of the cabin and . . . and well, here I am."

It wasn't as simple as that, she thought wryly. How to describe her shock when Edith had flung the envelope on the table before her, had told her she'd booked her in at the Waverley Hotel in Cape Town for a week so she'd have time to 'look around' and decide whether to stay in

Cape Town or travel all over Southern Africa, and that she'd booked her in for the next day, and until the ship sailed, at the Cumberland.

"You must snap out of this, Mary," Edith had said angrily. "You can lean on me now, but once you're out of England, you'll be on your own."

Mary smiled wryly as she sipped her cold drink. Somehow it hadn't worked out that way. She still had people to lean on. She had come on board the ship on a miserably cold grey day with the rain teeming down and her new suitcases filled with the most expensive and most beautiful clothes she had ever seen.

It seemed to her she was the only person to come on board alone. She had given up her ticket, been directed to her cabin and got lost in the endless and all-exactly-alike white corridors. She had stood there, a little frightened, feeling rejected by everyone when Dirk Paynton had come along.

"Can I help you?" he'd asked. "You look a little lost."

"I am more than a little," she confessed. "I can't find my cabin."

How he'd laughed and somehow it had made her feel less lonely. "We all get lost for the first few days," he told her. "Then we suddenly know which way we're going. Come along, I'll show you . . ."

She'd been glad Edith had got her a single cabin for she'd have hated to share it. In addition, it had a private bathroom and was quite large.

Dirk whistled softly as he looked round it. "Quite nice. But where's your husband going to sleep?"

"He isn't here . . ." she'd said and some of her loneliness, perhaps her unhappiness, must have got into her voice for Dirk looked at her quickly and said: "Let's go up and have a drink. We'd better introduce ourselves . . ."

That was how it all began. How glad she'd been to have Dirk by her side for the ship was full of couples or of families come to see the passengers off. It was noisy, with laughter and the popping of champagne corks.

Afterwards they went on deck to the incessant roar of the cranes and winches. They talked and watched the cranes lift their incredibly heavy loads of crates and luggage or cars and swing them in the air as they hung poised above the holds, and the men below waved their arms in signals or blew whistles. The noise never stopped. Visitors thronging the deck and people shouting and laughing, and suddenly Mary had known an absurd desire to rush to her cabin, grab her luggage and go ashore. Why was she doing this? she asked herself. Why? Why? Why?

Dirk, who seemed to have uncanny perception, had taken her arm and led her into the smoking room.

"Can't hear a word out there," he'd said cheerfully.

Looking round at the sandal-wood panelling that hid the bar, at the red-topped stools, the big armchairs and huge couches Mary tried to relax. It was too late to go back. Deep red carpet, a glowing electric fire, the crowd of people in the chairs. Gradually she'd regained her control and could talk to Dirk. She'd been glad to have his company that day.

And many days since, she thought, as

she finished her drink. Never had she felt so alone, so alien. So . . . so out on a bough. Now she knew what Edith meant when she said that a woman alone lived a tough life. Already she'd had passes made at her and it was obvious that many men thought a woman travelling alone was 'easy' and were annoyed when they found she wasn't.

But Dirk wasn't like that. He paid compliments, looked after her, made her think in many ways of Garth.

And Garth was the one person she didn't want to think about!

"So your friend suggested you take the trip, walk out of the picture for six months, so as to speak," Dirk said thoughtfully, "And then, when you did nothing, she stepped in and threw you out?"

Mary smiled. "No, she certainly didn't. She just gave me a gentle push."

"H'm. Sounds to me as if she wanted to get you out of the way. Could it be she has an eye on your husband?"

"If she has, she hasn't a hope . . . "

He lifted dark eyebrows. "You're very sure of yourself, aren't you? Not afraid of losing your husband . . . ?"

Suddenly she didn't want to talk about it. She'd told a half-truth. She was sure Garth would never look at Edith, he'd made that clear enough. What she wasn't so sure about, was . . . was 'that woman'.

She stood up. "I've got a migraine coming on," she lied. "See you later, Dirk."

"You can count on that . . . " He pushed his chair back and stood up, too. "Sure you won't get lost?"

"Sure." She smiled and walked along the deck, unaware that many eyes followed her tall, slender figure with the long perfect legs, and her head of amber-coloured hair, curled closely on top of her head, making her face even more ethereal-looking than ever, heightening the depth of her eyes, the cheekbones, that small, red, seductive mouth.

She was remembering that hasty impulsive visit to Garth's office. Try as she would to forget it, she couldn't.

Now she hurried below to her deck, along the corridor, into her cabin, closing the door, leaning against it, eyes tightly shut as her memory took her back.

She had been shopping for three days. Three surprisingly exciting days. The hairdresser had startled her by his skill, turning her long unwieldy hair into this light curly, easy-to-manage style, the beautician had also surprised her by teaching her how to make her eyes look even larger, how to make her skin glow, and show her how young she could look. Later, two interested young assistants had advised her about clothes, having, both told her, for they were friendly girls, a 'ball' of a time, for she had no need to worry about money. Some of the clothes she felt were too young but they had both disagreed and when, at the hotel, she had looked at her purchases, her first thought had been of Voi.

She'd been so tempted to phone Voi. But even as she lifted the telephone, she had known she couldn't. Voi's cruel words had hurt her terribly. None of them cared what happened to her, she'd told herself.

But next day she had dressed carefully. It had been a crisply cool Autumn day with a threat of rain and she had worn her fur coat and Cossack hat, a new exciting black wool dress with gold embroidery. She felt like a child, dressing up for a party.

So she had gone to see Garth. She had no idea why she wanted to see Garth — nor what she would say, she told herself. She only knew she *had* to see him. She was sailing the next day. She wanted him, she told herself, to see the new 'her', this young-looking, attractive 'her'. But that wasn't the whole truth, she'd known. The whole truth was that she had come to her senses. That she'd suddenly realised she had acted like a spoiled child, uncontrolled, unreasonable. It had all seemed so stupid, so futile, so . . . utterly ridiculous.

And so she'd gone to the office, wearing her dark glasses as protection, afraid of being recognised and Garth warned. She had stood there, waiting nervously, for the girl at the desk had said she would go and ask Mr. Herron's advice . . .

Then she had seen him. It was as if she had seen him properly for the first time. Perhaps it was the first time she had seen him with the eyes of a *woman*, and not those of a *wife*, or those of a frightened girl, aware that her father was shortly going to die.

This new Garth stood out. It was strange but she had never realised how handsome he was.

A door had opened and . . . and 'that woman' was there.

Looking just as she had at Bexhill station. Only she looked younger without a hat on. And she was saying something to Garth. She seemed terribly upset and Garth put his hand on her arm and bent down . . .

Mary had turned and hurried into the lift which had conveniently arrived at the right moment. And she had hurried out of the building, got a taxi and gone back to the hotel.

So it was true, she'd known Garth and this 'woman' were not just friends! She'd seen the way the 'woman' had looked up at him. Imploringly, yet sure of him. And the protective way he'd spoken to her, put his hand . . .

That was why Mary tried not to think of Garth any more. He had lied. She knew that, now. For sure.

She had come aboard, rejected, unloved, alone. But she wasn't alone any more. There was Dirk, then there was the handsome, red-bearded First Officer, Bruce Harvey, and Victor Courtney, the sophisticated, well-dressed man who was a bridge fiend but danced very well and seemed to seek her out, and there was also Adrian Greene.

But Adrian was different, of course.

She lay on her bed, closing her eyes and trying to relax. If only she could stop thinking about Garth and that . . . that woman!

How noisy ships were, she thought. Far noisier than she had imagined. Here in the cabin, it was never quiet. Constant creaking; in the night the strangest of bangs. Sometimes she woke up, frightened, lying very still, conscious of her aloneness. Then she'd switch on the light and make sure the cabin door was locked. And creep back to bed, feeling ashamed of herself. How childish could you be, she'd scold herself. But sometimes in daytime, too, even in the big lounge with its crowds of people, even here she knew moments of fear. What lay ahead? What was she going to do? If only someone would tell her . . .

She'd met Adrian one day when she'd escaped from Dirk and from Victor, for both wanted her to join in deck sports, and had gone to her favourite hiding place, right at the stern of the ship. Not on the upper deck but on one of the lower ones. It was pleasant there. Few people seemed to like it so she could usually get a deck-chair and sit by herself, watching that wide flat wash of water race behind them. She could sit for hours, not wanting to read or think, but just gazing as if mesmerised at the water.

"Fascinating, isn't it," a voice'd said and she'd turned and seen a man with fair, sandy-coloured hair, a face like a Greek god's and the unhappiest eyes she'd ever seen in her life.

"Yes," she'd said. "I can watch it for hours."

"I know. It stops one from thinking."

And so from that, they'd grown to know one another. His name was Adrian Greene. He was an electronics expert, and had his own business. He lived in

Edinburgh but was a Londoner, born and bred.

They rarely met. Usually at the stern of the ship, if both escaped there from their thoughts at the same time. One day he startled her by saying: "Are you waiting for a divorce?"

She swung round, angry and a little scared. "What makes you say that?"

He wasn't smiling. "Because you look the way I feel."

He'd told her he was waiting for his divorce to come through, that he loved his wife and he didn't know how he was going to live without her.

"Then why are you divorcing her?"

"I'm not. She's divorcing me."

"But . . . but why?"

As he told her the whole story, she thought how easy it was to confide in strangers on the ship. It was as if this was all unreal. Now as she listened to Adrian's story, she wondered how such a fine man could have been treated so badly by his wife.

"It's not her fault. She can't help being a nympho. Some people see the physical side of marriage as a token of love. I thought I showed my love by working hard to make a good living for Jenny and my kids. I must have been blind. I didn't see how lonely she was, how she began to believe I loved my work better than I loved her. I was a fool not to see that she wanted something warmer and more alive than just money . . . There've been other men but I looked the other way. I loved her, you see."

He spread out his hands and looked at them. Mary looked, too. He had the long fingers of a musician.

"I loved her. Then she had an affaire with my best friend. I would have looked the other way again but she told me she loved him and wanted to marry him so I let her divorce me . . . " He sounded tired.

"But why? You were innocent," Mary said at once.

And Adrian looked at her. "I love her. I don't want the children to know what she's like. They love her and need her. Kerr will make a good father but I'll miss them . . . "

"You'll see them?"

"I don't think so. I know I can but

. . . is it really fair? To the kids, I mean. That's why I've come out here. I think maybe I'll stay out here, build a new life, give them a chance to forget me. It must be tough on kids to have two fathers, two loyalties. I'd rather they forgot me. You've children?"

She had stared at him, trying to understand this man who loved his wife and could be so unselfish.

"Three," she told him, finding a strange pleasure in talking of them. She spoke of Voi and how difficult she could be, of her latest boy friend.

"An architect like my first love. Wasn't that odd?" she said and laughed.

"Did you marry your first love?"

"No . . . " she'd said and slid away from the danger of Garth's name. "Then there's Suzy. She's bright for her age. A little too bright, perhaps. Thinks she knows everything and is the only person with any sense in the world . . . "

They'd laughed together for Adrian had a son like that.

"When he's an 'oldie', he says, he's going to replan the world and make it fit to live in."

"Robbie is the youngest and . . . and very sweet," she said and realised that she meant it. She was remembering times when Robbie, trying not to cry, had raced into her arms and held her tightly. There was once when she was late and Mrs. White hadn't turned up and Robbie'd come home from school. He'd been much younger then, his first term at school, and the bus had dropped him off at the gates, and he'd found the house locked up and empty. Luckily Garth hadn't known about that! The second time it happened, Garth had discovered Robbie alone. How furious Garth had been. Quite frightening.

"I thought you'd gone for good . . . " Robbie had said that first time, clinging to her.

She could remember what she'd said, too. "I'll never go, Robbie."

But now she had.

It was so unfair for it wasn't her fault. Not really.

Now, as she lay on her bed, feeling the gentle movement of the ship, she thought of the children.

Adrian had made her buy postcards.

"The kids'll love 'em. I'm sending some."

"I thought you wanted them to forget you?" she'd said.

He looked at her. "Gradually, Mary, not all at once. I want to slowly fade away, not shock them by my disappearance."

Was that what she'd done? Mary wondered. She should have written more — not just that she was going away.

But what was there for her to say?

"Your father no longer loves me so I am going away to decide what to do."

That was the truth. So anything else would be a lie. But she could send cards now, and say she was having a wonderful time and send her love, couldn't she?

Quickly she showered, and dressed. She chose a simple white sheath frock, sleeveless and with a V neck. Already she was getting a slight tan. Everyone yearned for a tan on the ship. The first days out had been cold and wet and it was only after a miserably wet visit to Las Palmas that the sun had condescended to appear. But now it really was a sunshine cruise . . .

Patting her hair, she turned round before the glass. How much more fun it was to dress when you knew there were people to stare at you! And admire you! That was even nicer still, always allowing for the fact that they might not mean all the compliments they paid her!

She went along to the ship's shop and stared in the windows. There were some fascinating things there. A cowboy outfit Robbie would love. A 'medical' bag for Suzy, with a toy stethoscope and bandages. An elegant gold purse for Voi, And a really smashing, as Voi would say, suède jacket for Garth . . .

Shying away from the thought of him, she hurried into the shop, choosing cards and waiting her turn in the long line.

A big red-bearded man in white uniform came to stand by her side.

"Enjoying yourself?" he asked.

She nodded and looked up at him. Bruce was a handsome man, married and with six children. How could his wife bear to let him work on ships full of attractive women? Mary wondered. Was she eaten up with jealousy or could she trust him?

"I've been seeing some nice things for my children," she said. "Some fascinating things."

"Don't buy them on this trip. You'll see some more on the way home and plenty in the shops out here, too. It isn't a good idea to send the children too many gifts," he said, "They get blasé."

"I suppose so . . . " she agreed and paid for her cards, walking out with him, accepting his offer of a drink and going to the Lido with him. But deep inside her, something stirred. She didn't know or recognise it for what it was, but it was the first stirrings of revolt. For the first time, she resented advice. They were her kids. Why shouldn't she buy them presents if she wanted to? Why was it people always bossed her about? she found herself thinking, as she laughed and talked with him over their drinks.

That night there was a Fancy Dress Ball. Mary didn't dress up for it but she wore a black velvet gown with a long chiffon veil hanging down the back. It was a hot humid night and both Dirk and Victor, in turn, led her out on to the deck to admire the moonlit

186

sea, where each in turn leant over the railings next to her, a hand on her arm, fingers exploring the little hollow in her elbow, eyes watching her face. It amused her, rather, to let the hand reach her shoulder and then she would yawn and say she was thirsty and what about a drink? The disappointed face, the note of resignation in the man's voice, made her want to laugh. If this was what Edith meant by 'flirting,' Mary decided she liked it.

The longer she was on board the more relaxed she became, more able to enjoy the unnatural way of life. She was glad she had Dirk's company, and Victor to dance with, and Adrian to meet now and then, and Bruce to talk to. It kept her days full, her evenings pleasurable as they danced and drank and talked and laughed.

It was so completely different from anything she had ever experienced before. She didn't think she would like all her life to be like this but as the ship approached the African coast, she began to regret that the voyage was nearly over.

Quite a number of people on the ship were ill, though few were seasick for it was a gentle voyage, the sea controlled and beautiful. It was on the last day but one that she realised she hadn't seen Adrian for several days. On an impulse, she went down to their favourite retreat, but there was no Adrian sitting there, watching the wash as it sped away, widening the farther it went.

"Mary . . . I've been looking for you all over the ship," Dirk said, coming up behind her, putting his arm lightly round her shoulder.

She moved slightly so that his hand dropped to his side.

"I'm sorry. I was looking for a friend."

"Male?"

She laughed, tossing her head. "Of course."

His hand closed over her arm. "What would your husband say?"

"Who cares . . . " she asked and, for a moment, meant it. She was fast forgetting Garth and her problem. If he loved that woman and.wanted to marry her, well, why not, she told herself defiantly. She could easily marry again. No one need say 'Poor Mary,' any more!

"We land tomorrow," Dirk said. "I'm sorry."

Leaning against the rail she half turned to face him.

"So am I — for many things."

"I'm staying at the Rooseveldt . . . where are you?"

"Edith booked me in at the Waverley. I haven't a clue what it's like."

"The Waverley! You were lucky to get in. It's very popular and most expensive. But then money doesn't matter to you, does it."

"No. I'm lucky like that."

"You're lucky in so many ways. Young, beautiful, happily married . . . "

Was there a trace of sarcasm in his voice? Mary wondered.

"And I've got three lovely children," she finished.

But had she? she wondered, turning away, gripping the railing tightly as she gazed down into the blue-green sea with its flecks of white.

Had she lost them all, when Garth stopped loving her? Why had he stopped? Where had she gone wrong? she wondered.

At what moment did he stop loving her? If only . . .

"Time for a drink," Dirk said, taking hcr arm.

It was a hot day but the wind blew, whirling up the skirts of the thin summer frocks. Mary clung to hers as they made their way along to the Lido. People were still swimming, others sunbathing, the girls' elaborate hair styles looking almost comical above their brief bikinis.

"There are so many old people on board," Mary said. "Is this the sort of holiday an old person can enjoy?"

"Yes, for it's an escape from reality," Dirk said after he'd succeeded in gaining the attention of an overworked steward and ordered the drinks. "That's the attraction for us all. We're no longer a part of the world. We can forget our personal. responsibilities. Feel young and behave like idiotic adolescents . . . "

"I hope I haven't," Mary said stiffly.

He laughed. "Oh, no, my dear, you've behaved like the perfect English lady — of the Victorian era. What an influence your elderly parents had on your life. They've completely moulded you to their pattern. I doubt if you've ever really enjoyed yourself. Let down your hair, I mean." He laughed as her hand flew to her short hair. "I don't mean literally but I bet you've never done something you wanted to and said to hell with the consequences," he added, his voice bitter.

"My friend, Edith, said that, too . . . " Mary told him with a smile.

"I'm beginning to think your friend Edith had more sense than I gave her credit for." Dirk joined in the laughter but his eyes were watchful. "Still, one can always hope."

Mary wasn't listening. She looked round at the small tables crowded with passengers, at the rows of deck chairs out on the deck, all filled, then at a group of Portuguese who were playing cards and shouting excitedly, arguing with wild gestures.

"I hope he's all right . . . " she said slowly.

Dirk frowned. "Hope who's all right?"

"Adrian . . . " She turned to look at him. "Adrian Greene. Just someone, one of the passengers. I don't know him well but we sometimes meet on deck and . . . "

"For a casual acquaintance, you seem quite concerned."

"In a way, I am. He's so terribly unhappy, you see."

"He told you his life story, Mary, and made your heart bleed?" Dirk teased.

She didn't smile. "I can't get over it, Dirk. His wife walked out on him so he gave her a divorce, and he still loves her."

"What can't you understand?" Dirk signalled to a passing steward to refill their glasses.

Mary clasped her hands and looked at them. "It's hard to explain. How could you go on loving someone who's . . . who's rejected you?"

"How can you stop — if you really love them?"

Dirk's words startled her. She glanced up. "You could love someone like that?"

He smiled. "That is love." He offered her a cigarette. The ship was rolling a little as they drew nearer the Cape. "Of course you get over it, in time. Or at least, you fool yourself you do."

"Love . . . " Mary said very quietly. "Then . . . then if you really loved someone, you should forgive them everything?"

"Heavens above, Mary, you've got hold of the wrong end of the stick. Forgiveness doesn't come into it. Some one walks out on you. You're hurt. You're angry. Jealous. You could kill them . . . " He was talking quietly but there was a note of intensity in his voice that surprised her. He twisted his hands together, almost as if they were round someone's throat. "The point remains that if they come back, you'll be so glad. You love a person, not because they're faithful to you. Not because they're kind. You love them because . . . well . . . " He gave an odd little laugh. "Just because."

"Just . . . because . . . " Mary echoed.

She finished her drink quickly and stood up. "I've got a lot of packing to do, Dirk."

He stood up. "Of course. See you later."

Nodding, she hurried away. Down to a deck below and then outside. The rollers were white-flecked now, the ship in a definite swell. She walked unsteadily to the railings and leaned over them, gazing at the grey sea.

"Just because . . . " she echoed.

You love someone 'just because'. For no rhyme or reason, asking nothing, expecting nothing. Was that real love? she wondered. But that wasn't what she felt for Garth.

Had she ever loved him? she wondered unhappily. Had she merely rushed into marriage with him because he offered her the protection she was afraid of losing when her father died? Was that why she had loathed the physical side of marriage? Was it because she saw Garth as a father . . . and so making love became disgusting, a form of incest?

She shivered and began to walk down the deck, adjusting her movements to the rolling ship. Had she any idea what love was? she asked herself.

Dirk's violence had startled her. Even frightened her a little. He was such a sophisticated man, a little too sure of himself, she had sometimes thought. Yet under that veneer of . . . was it self-defence? — apparently lay this terrible pain, this rejected love of his. She wondered if he was married. Dirk never talked about his private life, always deftly changing the subject should it crop up. He was working, he'd told her, for one of the largest electrical firms in England, and hoped to arrange some very big sales. She'd no idea where he lived even.

Yet he could love someone, love them enough to go on loving that person no matter how hurt he was, how much he'd been cheated.

Was that the secret of her inability to trust Garth? she wondered. Her hatred of being cheated? Lied to? Then if that could make her able to walk out of his life, had it proved that she did not love Garth?

And if she didn't love him, then . . .

She turned away and hurried into the noisy ship, going down to her cabin, trying not to think about Garth.

She began to pack but her hands were all thumbs and in the end, she lost her patience and stormed out of the cabin. She could not forget Garth.

Tiny incidents flashed before her

memory like slides in a projector. Garth and his thoughtfulness that time she had fallen and sprained her ankle. Then his patience with her after Suzy's birth, when she went through a long period of depression which had taken months to overcome. Garth giving her a birthday gift, his face eager as he watched her unwrap the parcel. Garth — that tower of strength, on whom she could always rely.

Yet the first time he let her down . . .

Or appeared to let her down . . .

It had been impossible to forgive him!

Not only that. Far worse than that. She'd found it impossible to believe him!

The ship's shop was open, not quite so crowded as usual. She stood before the window and suddenly, she straightened herself and walked into the shop.

Half an hour later she staggered back to her cabin, her arms full of parcels. Goodness only knew where she'd pack them, she thought a little ruefully, but she'd manage it.

She laid them on the bed and looked at them, imagining young Robbie racing round in his cowboy suit, his gun at the ready. She saw Suzy bending over her dolls, the minute stethoscope hanging round her neck, while she listened to the doll's heart, a rapt look on her young face. She thought of Voi with the elegant gold mesh handbag. Now she'd need gold sandals to match it.

Then she stroked the soft suède of the jacket she'd bought Garth. How smooth it was. How elegant. She loved the colour, a warm claret red. She had hesitated about buying it and then she had decided. After all, Garth was still her husband and it was Christmas! It would suit him. Very well! Only, she realised suddenly, she wouldn't be there to see it.

Feverishly, she packed, suddenly hating being alone. She bathed and dressed quickly and went up to the cocktail bar. Victor was there and he came to meet her. A tall, well-built man with snow-white hair and a big nose and the warmest of smiles.

"My day is made, Mary," he said, leading her to a couch. "Usually that obnoxious creature, Dirk Paynton, has grabbed you first. Now what about a drink?"

"Thank you . . . " Mary was looking round at the different couples and groups, but there was no sign of Garth . . . then she felt her cheeks burning as she hurriedly sorted her confused thoughts. No sign of Adrian, she had meant to think.

When had she last seen him? she wondered. A few days back at one of the Captain's cocktail parties. He'd been alone. She'd been with Dirk. They'd waved to one another, but that was all. She wondered why she felt so worried.

Could she be falling in love with him, a small voice seemed to ask.

In love? With Adrian? Her hand shook as she lifted her glass and some of the amber-coloured liquid splashed on to her sea-green frock.

Victor leant forward and gently mopped it with his handkerchief. "Getting excited about arriving?"

It was an effort to focus her gaze properly on him, to remember who Victor was, to find the ability to speak to him.

"Yes. Of course . . . My first visit . . . "

"Is it, now? That's interesting. I've been living here for nearly fifteen years. I have a very charming little house. You must come round and have dinner with me sometime. Where are you staying? With friends?"

"No. At the Waverley Hotel. I don't know what it's like."

He pursed his mouth. "Not bad. Not bad at all. I must show you some of the beautiful countryside. It really is lovely."

"I'm sure it is."

Mary had just seen Dirk. He was standing by the bar, arms folded, a scowl on his face, as he stared at her. She smiled and waved and then looked at Victor. A warm sense of security filled her. She wasn't alone. Both these men found her attractive. A comforting — and also exciting — thought. What would Edith say? she wondered. At least, Edith'd have to admit that poor Mary was no longer 'poor Mary', a cabbage, merely existing. That was one thing she was doing now, Mary told herself, at least she 'lived'.

★ ★ ★

There was a long queue next morning as the passengers lined up for the Immigration Authorities. Mary shifted her weight from foot to foot, trying to get a glimpse through the huge windows at the fabulous mountain that dominated the scene. She had been up early to finish her packing and had come up on deck as the ship slowly came into dock. The huge mountain, crouching above the buildings scattered in the valley below, had been half hidden by clouds. The sun had been hot even at that hour and then it had been time to have breakfast quickly so as to get into the queue early. But nearly everyone had had the same thought and the queue seemed to stretch ahead endlessly. She turned her head and found herself gazing into Adrian's pale face.

"Adrian," she said impulsively. "I've been so worried about you. I haven't seen you for days."

He smiled. "That's the nicest thing you could say — that you noticed I wasn't around. Actually, I've been sick. One of these wretched tummy maladies that leave you so terribly weak . . . "

As the queue moved slowly forward, they talked. He asked her where she was staying and when she said the Waverley, he made a face.

"Stuffy. Full of millionaires who bore one to death. I'm staying with the friend of a friend. I hear he runs a very unusual type of hotel. How long are you booked in for?"

"I'm not sure. My friend, Edith, booked it for me."

"Of course. I remember you telling me. Had any letters?"

"Are they on board? I didn't think of looking. Have you?"

"Yes. I'm a free man . . . " he said, but the joke misfired and although he turned away quickly, she saw the misery in his eyes.

They were silent for a while. Mary trying to imagine how she would feel if a letter came saying that Garth had divorced her. Only he wouldn't, of course, even if he could. Garth would let her divorce him. Just as Adrian had done. In many ways, the two men were much alike.

At last the passports had been examined and stamped, the luggage had gone and it was time to tip the stewards, make sure nothing was left, and go ashore.

Mary went on deck and felt, as she had done when she came on the ship, most horribly alone. People were leaning over the rails, shouting and waving to the masses of people on the docks, who were waving and shouting in return.

She felt lost, absurdly helpless, as she hesitated by the gangway and then a warm hand held her elbow and Victor said:

"My car'll be here, waiting for me, so I'll drive you to the hotel. First we have to go through Customs. Got much to declare?"

"I don't know . . . What do I have to declare?"

Victor smiled. "I see you're used to having a man around." He led the way down the gangway, turning to talk to her, as he explained the requirements of the Customs official. "I expect they'll take one look at you and chalk your cases. It's men like me they delight in harassing. D'you mind waiting if I get held up?"

"Of course not. It's awfully nice of you to give me a lift . . . " Mary said, her depression lifting.

Victor was right. The Customs official asked a few questions, smiled and chalked her cases. She found a seat and waited, watching Victor enter into a spirited argument with a short, fat official. Finally, his cheeks flushed, Victor joined her, got a porter and led the way to his car.

It was a large cream car. The coloured porter put the cases in the vast boot and the coloured chauffeur drove them away from the docks. Table Mountain was still shrouded by clouds, but everything fascinated Mary as she looked at the bright clusters of purple flowers scrambling up the sides of white houses, at the gardens ablaze with colours, at the palm trees, tossing their long fronds in the breeze.

The hotel was vast. Rather too aggressively luxurious, she thought. Victor supervised her entry, checking that the booking was in order, going with Mary up in the lift to the eighth floor, inspecting the large room with its wide bed draped in white chiffon, its french windows opening on to a balcony that overlooked the blue sea.

"You should be comfortable, here," Victor said and smiled. "May I come round and see you?"

"Please do." Mary smiled gratefully. "And thank you so much for looking after me. I did feel a bit lost . . . "

"My pleasure . . . " he said and then he was gone.

And she was alone.

How big the room was and empty. Her luggage had been dumped, the porter saying there would be a maid along soon. Mary went out on to the balcony and the full heat of the sun hit her. But it was lovely. Really lovely.

Unfortunately scenery, no matter how beautiful, is no substitute for companion-ship, she soon discovered. After the social life on the ship and the constant attentions of Dirk and Victor, not to forget the stimulating conversations with the First Officer and the occasional meetings with Adrian, life was suddenly very sterile. Drab. Bare. Miserable!

She had lunch and felt very much alone in the crowded dining-room.

Afterwards she put on a thin dress, pale blue cotton, and went out into the sunshine. The hotel was not far from the shops and she bought herself a sunshade and a fan, as well as brown paper and string for she wanted to send off the parcels.

Back at the hotel, the packing gave her something to do. She put small notes inside the parcels. 'With love from Mum'. In Garth's, she put nothing. What was there to say?

She sat on the balcony and stared at the deep blue sea, the yachts far out with their vivid red and candy-striped spinnakers. She looked down at the swimming pool and the people lying around it. Just like on the ship.

But with one big difference. Here she was alone.

Tempted to stay in her room and order dinner to be brought to her yet somehow she felt the room had become a prison. That was rather amusing, for, if it was a prison cell, it must be the most luxurious in the world, she thought. The carpet was cream, from wall to wall. The curtains the softest of azure blue silk. There were mirrors everywhere. In the bathroom, all the walls were mirrors.

She wore a long gown of black chiffon and went down to dinner. The head waiter led her to a small table tucked away behind a pillar. The waiter came, resplendent in white trousers, a red cummerbund and red fez, and a short white jacket. When she had finished her dinner, she sat for a long while, absurdly afraid of getting up alone and walking by herself, knowing that everyone's eyes would watch her progress. Curious eyes, assessing the price of her frock, of the emerald necklace round her neck with matching ear-rings. Criticising her way of walking, the hair style, her body. She gave a little shudder. Why did a woman alone feel so terribly vulnerable? she wondered. Why did she have this fear of being stared at and ridiculed?

At last she stood up and managed to walk out of the room. In the hall, she hesitated. It was too early to go to bed and yet, where could she go alone?

In the end, she went up to her bedroom. Standing out on the balcony, she could see the twinkling bright lights of the town, the distant flashes of a lighthouse. How dark it got here, so much earlier than in England, she thought. Then she imagined the cold autumn in England, with its yellow fogs and heavy rain, while here . . . She lifted her head and the warm evening air seemed to caress her cheeks. This was lovely, she told herself.

Then a mosquito bit her. And another. And another. Moths were fluttering around and she went hastily back into her bedroom, closing the screen doors, standing there. Wondering what to do. Alone.

Garth

GARTH shivered as he came out of the warmth of the Underground into the wet street. What a horrible night! It matched his mood perfectly as he hurried across the road with the scores of other hurrying workers, homeward bound. He hated the thought of the lonely hours ahead. It had been a bad day, although it was difficult to pin-point what had made it so. He tried to believe it was his imagination but at the office he felt as if he was disliked. Even as if he'd been sent to Coventry for being the cause of Carol's departure! At times, he had the feeling that the young girls avoided him, as if scared lest he make a pass at them and they be given the sack!

How he hated these cold wet days and the evenings that dragged interminably. There was something so impersonal about a bed-sitter, for that was all his so-called furnished flat actually was.

He hurried up Church Street and turned off into the Grove. When he saw the light burning in his sitting-room, he was conscious of mixed sensations. Mainly they were of relief for that meant Carol was there. He'd go into a warm flat, the electric fire glowing cheerfully, his drink ready on the table by his chair, and a delicious smell of cooking. Carol's working hours were different from his, now, and she nearly always hurried straight to his flat, cooked his meal, welcomed him home and had a quick drink with him before rushing off to Victoria to catch her train back to Bexhill.

He had often asked her not to do it. "You'll get so tired . . . "

She had just laughed.

Now as he opened the front door and climbed the two flights of steep stairs, he felt warmed and happy at the thought of the welcome that awaited him. His key was hardly in the lock before the door was flung open and she was there.

"What a night!" she said, grabbing his wet umbrella and his brief case. "Come in. You look soaked . . . "

"And you look lovely," he said simply and then wished he'd kept his mouth shut as he saw the joy on her face.

"Do I?" She looked down at the dark green pinafore frock of wool with the white blouse. "It's nice and warm."

He closed the door. "You always look so nice and clean . . ."

Carol laughed and led the way.

The two drinks were ready. She sat on a low stool close to the electric fire and smiled up at him.

"Tough day?"

He nodded. "They treat me as if I had leprosy."

"Oh, Garth, I wish you didn't have this . . . this sensitivity," she said with a seriousness she rarely showed. "It's not your fault that I had to leave the firm. It's your father's fault for making that rule and the partners' faults for keeping it up. We did nothing wrong so there's nothing to feel ashamed about."

He put out his hand and stroked her hair. How soft it was!

"Maybe I shouldn't have got into the habit of travelling with you on the train . . . maybe . . ."

"Maybe . . . !" Carol caught hold of his hand and laid it against her cheek. "Can't you see how happy I am, Garth? You've given me something I've not had for years. The chance to look after the man I love. Maybe women are queer cattle, as you say, but there's just one thing we're all alike in. We love looking after the men we love. You can't imagine what pleasure it gives me to rush here from work, have a warm welcome for you when you come back, even if I do have to rush off at once . . . " She looked at her watch and sighed. "I must be on my way."

He went with her to the door, helped her into her white raincoat, smiled as she adjusted the small souwester cap.

"Carol . . . " he began and hesitated. "It's just that I don't want you to get hurt."

"Garth. I began to get hurt when . . . when I first met you. I loved you from the beginning. I can't be hurt any more. Honestly, Garth, I'm so happy . . . Oh, dear . . . I must fly."

He pulled a note from his pocket. "Carol, have a taxi tonight. There'll be

211

some about in Church Street . . . I don't want you to get wet . . . "

She pushed the note back into his hand and smiled. "All right — I'll have a taxi if I see an empty one. Not to worry. I'm used to the rain. See you tomorrow . . . oh, by the way, the sauce will need warming. Otherwise everything's ready."

"Thanks . . . "

He watched her hurry down the stairs. He leaned over the rail and from the hall she waved to him. Then he went into the flat, closed the door and walked quickly to the window, pulling back the curtain, gazing down at the rain-splashed street, seeing her hurry out of the house, put up her umbrella and run down the street.

A tall man moved out from the doorway of a shop, glanced up at the house, and then set off down the road behind Carol.

Garth caught his breath and then let the curtains fall. He turned to face the empty room. Suppose . . . just supposing someone had advised Mary to have him watched, to seek evidence? If it was proved that Carol came to his flat every single evening ... ?

He swallowed his drink quickly and refilled the glass. Then he switched on the T.V. and sat down, not looking at it, but welcoming the noise and voices as companions.

It was all so fantastically stupid. From the beginning, it had been an innocent relationship. He had liked Carol, found her amusing and interesting, enjoying companionship on the long train journeys he loathed, and which he did simply because Mary wanted to live at Little Common. What worried him was that Carol was so involved. She could tell him a thousand times that it wasn't his fault, that she'd fallen in love with him, but then, if he hadn't sought her out, got to know her better, she would have forgotten all about him long ago.

He drained the glass and got wearily to his feet. What was frightening him now was the fact that, fight it as he might, he was beginning to fall in love with Carol. Two married people with all the complications and heartbreak that their union would involve! How could Carol divorce a man she can't trace? How could he divorce Mary and break the children's hearts?

In the tiny kitchen, he warmed the sauce, and dished up his veal and cauliflower. Carol was making him give up potatoes because he was putting on weight! Something Mary would never have thought of in a thousand years.

Mary! Sitting in his chair, one eye on T.V. where cops were chasing criminals across the screen, Garth thought about Mary. By now she must be nearly in Africa. He wondered what sort of voyage she'd had, if she'd made friends, if she'd been sea sick. Probably she was writing regularly to Edith but surely, surely it wasn't too much to ask? — surely she could have written to the kids? So far, he'd managed to fend off their complaints by saying Mummy was on the high seas so she couldn't write, but what could he say if the months passed by and she still didn't write? What a strange creature Mary was. Wrapped in self-interest and self-pity. She had no interest in anyone else, no sympathy for them, no tolerance or understanding. Poor Mary. It wasn't her fault but still, it didn't make it any easier to live with her. Why, not even in their early days of marriage, had Mary ever given him the sort of welcome Carol gave him every night. Somehow Mary wasn't the kind who 'gives'. She only 'took'.

He washed up and put the china and silver away. Then switched off the T.V. and opened his brief case. He looked through the papers and tried to forget his troubles in his work.

But the evening dragged on and on. He found himself thinking again. Remembering.

Mary — when he first met her. The shy, frail-looking girl who had thought him so wonderful. How he had loved her need for him, her dependence on him. Never had he wanted to depend on her — yet now, he was moaning because she had never made a fuss of him! Carol was the kind of woman who loved making a fuss of you, who took a real pride and joy in doing it.

He began to walk round the room. This sort of life couldn't go on indefinitely. He knew that. It had to end. If he wasn't very careful, he'd finish up by being deeply in love with Carol and then there'd be real trouble.

The next night was dry but crisply cold, his breath showing on the night air as he hurried back to his small flat. He glanced up as soon as he turned into the Grove and something seemed to jolt inside him.

There was no light on.

He walked up the two flights of stairs and let himself in, switching on the light. Shivering as he took off his coat. He went and switched on the fire, warming his hands, How cold and drab everything was. He poured himself a strong drink, then a second one. Went to the kitchen and investigated the fridge. There was a pork chop there and some eggs, so he wouldn't starve!

Going back to the sitting-room, he sat down, turning the glass restlessly in his hands, his eyes constantly going to the door as he silently willed it to open.

He began to prowl around the room restlessly. Going every now and then to the window, pulling back the heavy curtains to look down the well-lit street. But no Carol hurried along the pavement.

It was then he began to worry. Perhaps she was ill. Could she have caught a chill the night before? Or she could have been in an accident! The trouble was he never saw her nowadays during the day. He went to the phone and stopped himself. How could he explain his call to her mother? Had the old lady any idea of what was happening? Or did she merely think Carol worked longer hours in this job?

Suddenly the lies and deceits sickened him. It wasn't right that a girl like Carol . . .

He stood very still. So this was it, was it? he asked himself. He *was* falling in love with Carol!

There was only one thing to do. He went quickly to the phone. Luckily he got through right away.

"Could I speak to Miss Herron?" he asked the impersonal voice that replied.

He had to wait a while and then Voi answered.

"Why, Dad?" She sounded surprised. "Everything all right?"

"Yes, darling," he said, trying to speak lightly. "You remember you rang me up some time back, soon after I moved in here, and you said you'd been thinking about what Suzy said . . . I mean about you coming to live with me so that I could be looked after?" He managed a laugh but it wasn't a very good one.

"Well . . . ?" There was a cagey note in Voi's voice. He wondered, then, if she'd rather not live with him! "I was thinking it would be rather nice if you did. You know, Voi, I get pretty lonely sometimes."

"You do?" She sounded surprised and then her voice changed, became warm. "Oh, Daddy darling, it's just that you're not used to being on your own. I'd love to come and be with you. Shall I give notice? I mean, I guess, I'll have to stay here until the end of the term . . . "

"Tell them I'll pay for you but . . . but I'd rather you came here soon," he told her hurriedly. "Say . . . say next week?"

"Of course, Dad. You're sure everything's all right?"

"Sure. Quite sure, darling. Just that . . . "

"I know," she said.

He had the strange feeling that she did.

Was she still eating her heart out for love of Bob? He was suddenly filled with the desire to tell her the truth about Bob and then stopped. There was nothing she could do and no sense in upsetting her still more.

"Thanks, darling . . . " he said and as he put down the receiver, the front door opened and Carol was there, laden with a full shopping basket, an apologetic smile on her face.

"Sorry I'm late, darling, but I had to work overtime. Case of panic in the office . . . " she stopped and stared at him. "Are you all right? You look upset."

He took the heavy shopping basket from her. "I was worried about you."

"Were you?" she said. Perhaps it was the wistful note in her voice. Perhaps the way she looked at him. Perhaps it was simply that suddenly he had to do something he'd wanted to do for a long time.

He dropped the shopping basket and took her in his arms. She clung to him, her mouth warm on his. It was a long moment before he let her go.

"I'm sorry, Carol."

She laughed, almost gaily. "I'm not. I've been hoping you would . . . "

"But Carol, it can lead nowhere . . . "

"I know . . . I know . . . " she took the shopping basket to the kitchen and began to empty it, putting the tins away, the frozen foods in the fridge "I know, Garth," she said over her shoulder, "I know you're in love with your wife."

"Look, Carol . . . "

She tossed him a piece of paper. "That's two pounds fifteen and fivepence halfpenny, darling, that you owe me for this food. Better check. I got you some chipolata sausages for breakfast and . . . "

"Carol . . . " He took her by the shoulders and looked down at her, saw the moistness of her eyes, the sudden tremor of her mouth. "Oh, my darling . . . " he said and held her close. "I can't forgive myself . . . I've no right . . . "

She kissed him. "Don't spoil things, Garth. I've got so little. Don't take that away from me. Now, go and sit down while I cook you something. I've got to rush or Mother will be really worried . . . "

Obediently he went back to the sitting-room. He sat down, hands linked between his knees. He loved Carol . . . But did he? Really? He put his face in his hands and sighed. Was she right? Was he still in love with Mary? All he knew was that if he wasn't very careful, a lot of people were going to be hurt.

He heard noises from the kitchen then she joined him. Her face was flushed, her eyes reddened. He stared at her anxiously. Had he made her cry?

"Carol, we must talk about it," he said.

"What is there to say? We've said it."

He moistened his dry lips. "Carol, Voi rang me tonight and she . . . she wants to come and live with me."

There was dismay on Carol's face. Dismay she tried to hide and failed in doing. "Live . . . here? Then . . . "

"I know. But we can still meet, Carol . . . She . . . "

Carol looked at her watch. "Yes, I

see, Garth. You don't need to explain. It's a good idea. She'll enjoy looking after you."

She turned to go to the front door and put on her brown coat. He hurried to help her.

"Carol, I'm sorry," he said. "So sorry."

Gently she touched his cheek.

"So am I, darling. Goodbye . . . "

"No . . . " he said suddenly firm. "It needn't be goodbye. Voi isn't coming till next week. Couldn't we have this week . . . ?"

Suddenly she was in his arms and he felt the wetness of her tears on his cheeks.

"Yes, darling," she said against his mouth as she held him close. "We'll have this week . . . "

And then she was gone, running down the stairs, not pausing to look back.

He stood by the window and watched her hurry down the street. No tall man moved out of the shadows of the shop doorway to follow her, this time.

Garth went on standing there, long after she was out of sight. And then he turned back to the empty room.

At least, he told himself, he had until the end of the week.

* * *

The next night, Carol was waiting for him when he got home, the flat full of the warm smell of onions frying. They sat down by the electric fire and talked. Of this and that; of Carol's new job which she found quite exciting, of his, and of his feeling of being ostracised. Carol leant against his knees and his fingers gently ran through her soft hair. He was beginning to regret his impulsive action in asking Voi to come and live with him. He knew he would miss these few moments alone with Carol. That was the trouble, of course, he told himself. Each time he saw her, he hated the thought of never seeing her again even more than before.

The buzzing of the front door bell startled them both. Garth hesitated and Carol laughed.

"Whoever it is, knows you're in, darling. They can see the light."

Reluctantly and resentful of the

interruption, Garth lifted off the small receiver. "Yes?" he said curtly.

He was startled to hear his daughter's voice.

"Dad, I must talk to you. It's terribly important."

"Voi! Darling, of course. Come right up . . . " He pressed the button that would open the front door and turned to Carol, who was now sitting in a chair by the electric fire. "It's Voi. She's upset about something. I had to . . . "

Carol smiled. "Of course you had to, Garth. Not to worry. Everything's all right. I'm just an old friend who pops in to cook a meal to help you out and who won't be needed once Voi takes over."

He looked at her sharply but there was no malice in her smile, simply an acceptance of a fact.

The front door of the flat was open with Garth standing there anxiously, as Voi came running up the stairs. She was well wrapped up against the cold but she looked upset.

"Sorry about this, Daddy, but I had to ask you," as he tried to draw her inside, she went on: "I've simply got to know about Bob . . . "

"Bob? Why . . . " he began and saw that she had just seen Carol. "Come in, darling," he said hastily. "I want you to meet an old friend of mine, Carol Stirn . . . Carol, this is my daughter . . . "

He helped Voi out of her sheepskin-lined green nylon coat. She hardly moved, staring like a zombie and then, as Carol stood up and came forward, hand extended, Voi seemed to come alive.

"I'm sorry," she said to Carol. "I'm afraid I'm . . . I'm not with it, at the moment. I've just had rather a shock and . . . " Carol shook hands. "Come and sit down and let your father get you a drink. It's cold, isn't it . . . I met your young brother. Robbie."

Voi smiled. If you could call it a smile. She was obviously struggling to be polite. "Oh, yes, I remember. You've got twins and he couldn't get over the fact that one was tall and one was short."

Carol laughed. "I know, but, you see, they're not identical twins. They're completely different, too, in every way . . . Sit here . . . " She pulled another chair up close to the fire and sat down herself. "I've wanted to meet you for a long time. And Suzy . . . "

"Oh, Suzy's the bright one of the family," Voi said, "At least she thinks so . . . "

Carol laughed and glanced at her watch. "I've only five minutes left, I'm afraid."

"You've got to go . . . " Voi glanced at her father as he handed her a drink. "I'm sorry if I interrupted . . . "

He smiled and sat down. "On the contrary, I'm very glad to see you, darling," he lied. "Carol always has to go at this time and it's lonely without her. She cooks my dinner for me every night. It's very good of her for then she has to rush to Victoria to catch her train to Bexhill . . . "

Voi looked at him. "I see," she said and he wondered, with a sudden chilly fear, just how much she did see. "That's why you asked me . . . "

There was a little silence that seemed to fill the room as Garth looked round wildly, ashamed to look at Carol. It was Carol who saved the situation.

"Yes, Voi. You see, with nights of fog and frost coming, I won't always be able to come and cook your father's meal for him and you know what men are. He'd either go out and eat which costs a lot of money or starve . . . "

Voi laughed. "He'll probably starve to death with my cooking." Then she seemed to forget Carol for she turned to her father. "Dad, I know I stopped you telling me before but . . . but I've simply got to know. I was too proud to ask you about Bob but . . . but I've got to know . . . " she repeated urgently.

"Today I went down to Esher. I knew Bob's parents lived somewhere near there. I didn't want to see them in case . . . in case he was there and didn't want to see me but . . . well, I met the Vicar in the church and . . . and he said it was very sad . . . and he said . . . he said Bob *was* a fine lad. Dad, is Bob dead? The Vicar said he didn't know. What did he mean?"

Garth leaned forward and took hold of her hands. "No, Voi, he isn't dead but . . . "

"But . . . ?" she whispered.

Garth drew a deep breath. "Look, Voi, he's in hospital and there's a chance he'll be quite all right but . . . "

Her face flamed with anger. "I'm not a child, Dad. All these 'buts'. I can take the truth."

"Well, he's in a coma, darling. The accident happened the day after he stayed with us. Remember he said his boss was taking him to see some house?"

"Yes, and I thought he was lying . . . "

"I thought so, too," Garth admitted. "I didn't blame him, wanting to get away."

They stared at one another.

"I know, I know," Garth said. "It was as much my fault as your mother's. You don't need to rub it in. Anyway, apparently the car went into a lorry. Bob's boss was killed outright and Bob is still in a coma."

Voi jumped up and went to the window, talking over her shoulder. "And I thought he'd just brushed me off. I didn't trust him . . . "

Garth went and stood by her side, his hand on her arm.

"Darling, this happens to us all. It's

not always easy to trust people."

She swung round. "But it should be, Dad. If you really love a person . . . " She looked across the room at Carol, who was standing, putting on her thick cream coat, collecting her things. "Don't you agree, Mrs. Stirn?"

Carol gave a little smile. "I do agree — in theory, Voi, but after all, we're only human, you know. It's easier sometimes to doubt the one you love. I'm sorry but I must rush. G'bye, both of you . . . " she said and hurried out of the room, slamming the front door behind her.

Voi turned to her father. "Dad, will Bob be all right?"

He gave a little shrug, drew back the curtains and watched Carol hurrying down the road. She glanced over her shoulder and waved. He waved back, let the curtains fall and turned to his daughter.

"Voi, I don't know. Neither do the doctors. But they say there's every hope. As far as they can discover, no physical damage has been done. The main trouble is . . . "

"His mind? He might be a cabbage . . . "

Voi's voice collapsed and her face crumbled as she sank into the chair, her hands pressed to her face. "Oh, my poor Bob . . . if only there was something I could do."

"There is, plenty," her father said curtly. He refilled her glass. "First, pull yourself together for tears won't help Bob."

Startled, Voi lowered her hands and stared at him. The mascara and tears had combined to form little black trickles down her cheeks. "But what can I do?"

"Help his parents. They're elderly and very upset. I've been in touch with them and have been to see Bob in hospital. He's at the Royal Weymouth in Monmouth Street . . . "

"You've been to see Bob . . . " Voi said slowly. "And you didn't tell me?"

"For heaven's sake! I tried to tell you and you made a scene in a public restaurant, storming out of the place like someone demented, making it obvious to me that I'd walked where angels fear to tread and you wanted to hear no more . . . "

Voi nodded. "You're right. It was

my fault, Daddy. I was a fool. If I'd
. . . But . . ."

"Look, Voi. I've often wondered since
if I should tell you but something stopped
me. Bob wouldn't want you rushing
around after him just because you're
sorry for him. You had to love him."

She nodded again. "You're right,
Dad."

"You see, Bob may be ill for a long
time, perhaps for ever. It would be a
great test for your love. I wasn't sure
I wanted that sort of life for you. I
thought that it was perhaps best if you
didn't know. The one thing Bob would
resent would be pity."

"But what can I *do*?"

"Ring his parents, ask after him, tell
them the truth. That I hadn't told you.
They may be wondering why Bob's
wonderful girl friend has disappeared
from the picture. Tell them it's my
fault and why I did it. Tell them you
were worried about him and found out
the truth. They'll love you for that. I think
they'd be glad if you'd share the hours of
sitting by his side with them. Someone
has to, all the time. In case he recovers

consciousness. He needs someone by his side, whom he can recognize."

"But . . . but . . . "

"Voi. That boy loves you. When I drove him to the station, he told me he knew you were very young but that nowadays people married young and he could afford to support a wife. I was . . . well, rather touched, for it's rare nowadays for a young man to talk to the girl's father. I also liked the way he spoke about you. He wasn't sure how you felt about him . . . "

"Oh, Daddy . . . " Voi stopped, her voice uneven.

"It won't be easy, Voi, I warn you. Sitting by the side of the unconscious body of someone you love for hours on end, isn't easy. Visiting a hospital daily is tough . . . "

"It's better than not seeing him at all, Daddy. And I am, really, very tough."

He smiled. "Good, then start showing me your toughness by dishing up the dinner for me. I've got a business phone call to make . . . "

He made the call, hearing his daughter's movements in the kitchen, hoping things would be all right, that Voi could be happy.

It was a pleasant dinner and he and Voi chatted, both shying away from the subjects of Bob and Carol. Several times, Garth was tempted to talk to her about Carol but he hesitated. He was afraid Voi might see how close to falling in love with Carol, he was.

Just as Voi was leaving, she looked at her father.

"Know something, Dad? I blamed Mum for Bob's silence. I can't help wondering how often we blame her for things that aren't her fault, at all."

It was a thought that stayed with Garth after Voi had gone.

Was it all Mary's fault? he asked himself. How many wives would have believed his story of his friendship with Carol? It had been an innocent friendship, but . . .

Had been? It still was, in actual fact. But wasn't it somewhere said in the Bible that to look at a woman with lust was the same as committing adultery? Did he look at Carol with lust? he wondered. It was a question he found hard to answer.

He tried to explain to Carol the next evening.

"Yes, I did ask Voi to come and share with me," he told Carol frankly. "I was getting worried . . . "

"But there's nothing to worry about, Garth," Carol said, her face distressed. "I love you. You can't change that. I know . . . I know there's no hope for us but . . . "

He caught hold of her and kissed her. "I'm afraid for me, Carol. Get that into your head. I'm falling in love with you and I don't want to . . . it's too complicated, too many people will be hurt."

Her eyes were sad. "Love is something you can't help."

"I don't agree," he said, pushing her away almost violently. "You can control it."

Carol turned away and straightened a book on the shelf. "Why not face the truth, Garth," she said. "You're attracted by me. I fill the empty space in your life, I'm like a mother to you, fussing, welcoming you home, caring for you but really, there's only one woman in your life. And that's Mary."

"But is she?" he asked. "Do I love her? Sometimes I wonder . . . "

She gave a strange smile. "Don't we all, at times? I love my husband — but I love you, also. Two quite different kinds of love. Maybe it's the same with you. You love your wife one way, and me another way."

"You still love your husband? Even after the way he's treated you?"

Carol laughed. "What has that to do with it? If he walked in tomorrow, I'd open wide my arms. That's love."

"Yet you say you love me? I don't get it."

She sighed, went close to him, rubbing her hand gently down his face. "I love you because you need me, Garth. Because you're lost and bewildered. I love you because you're kind and because you're handsome. I love you because you're you."

"But I thought the way you always knew you loved a person was because he or she was the only person in the world that mattered?"

"Of course. If they're around. It's when

they're not around, that you can love someone else."

"You mean, then, that if your husband walked in, now, you'd walk out of my life and forget me?"

"Walk out of your life, yes. But I'll never forget you. Garth."

She smiled at him.

"Don't let's spoil our last few chances to be alone together to talk about love, Garth. Let's just enjoy them. I told Mother I'd be late home tonight so I've got an extra hour. I've cooked dinner for both of us, too, so what about a bottle of champagne . . . "

"I haven't any."

She laughed. "I bought some. Let's celebrate our friendship which we'll never forget . . . "

He was no longer listening. He caught hold of her and held her close, kissing her.

"Oh, darling . . . " he was murmuring. "If only . . . "

Voi

VOI stared at the postcard in her hand. It said the same as the cards sent to Suzy and Robbie. She turned it over slowly. There was a picture of Table Mountain. That was the only difference, for their cards had been pictures of the ship. She put it on the bookshelf and got on with her work, in too great a hurry to think much about her mother's postcard though Voi was conscious of relief that she'd also got a card. Of course, hers had been delayed because it was forwarded from the Hostel, but already Suzy and Robbie had written excitedly to say they'd heard from 'Mummy'.

"Having a wonderful time, Love, Mummy."

Those were the words on all the cards. They told a lot and yet they told nothing. When she'd had no card, Voi had been afraid her mother was still angry with her.

Now as she hurried to prepare her father's evening meal Voi forgot about the card, her mother and everything but the fact that Bob was lying in the hospital ward asleep — or rather, looking as if he was asleep. That was the heartbreaking part.

Hastily she pulled on her coat, her new, gay red balaclava helmet, tucking her long hair inside it, and pushed her feet into her new, wool-lined long boots.

She ran down the stairs and out into the frosty night, hurrying down Church Street towards the Underground station. It was her evening to sit with Bob. The train was warm and she undid her coat. As she was jolted along, she wondered if her mother would write to Dad. Of course, that might be delayed, too, if it was sent to his hotel address.

It was quite a long walk to the hospital and Voi hurried a little. Bob's parents, two of his uncles and three of his cousins, and now Voi, had drawn up a roster so that one or other of the family was always by Bob's side.

Apparently the doctors had said it

was absolutely essential that, when Bob recovered consciousness, he should have someone he could recognise by his side. Whatever happened, he must not be allowed to come round and find himself alone, or surrounded by strangers.

Voi had been only too glad to offer her services and often she took time off from the College, but she also took her books with her and while sitting by Bob, she would practise her shorthand, or study. They were long hours to sit silently, staring down at his peaceful face and closed eyes, fighting the fear that never quite left her.

Now, as she hurried into the hospital, the visitors, queueing up for the moment when they could surge up to the wards like a river in flood, glanced at her enviously as she hurried up the stairs. The Staff was just in the ward, and she smiled at Voi and then, in answer to Voi's unspoken question, shook her head sadly.

"No change, I'm afraid, but . . . " She smiled at Voi, "There's always hope, my dear."

Voi hurried down the ward, aware

of the curious and sympathetic glances from the men sitting up in their beds, all awaiting eagerly the moment the doors would open and their visitors come surging in.

One of Bob's cousins, a pretty girl called Nesta, came out from behind the curtains to meet Voi. She looked tired.

"Hi," she said in a friendly voice. "Who's taking over from you?"

"Uncle Joe," Voi said for Bob's family had somehow become her family now, and all accepted her.

"Goodoh. He's the punctual type. Whew . . . " she whistled softly. "Am I sleepy. Don't you find it hard to stay awake?"

Voi's hand was on the curtain. She couldn't bear to leave Bob alone for a few seconds, even. "It isn't easy," she agreed.

She took off her coat and her balaclava and sat down on the hard chair by the bed. Bob lay as he had always done. She tried not to look at the various tubes going into his veins, the oxygen ready by his side.

"It won't be easy," her father had said

in the beginning. How right he'd been. Sitting here, listening to the laughter and talk from beyond the curtains, but being imprisoned here in silent helplessness, looking at Bob . . . dear Bob . . .

Hastily Voi bent down and drew her books and papers from the locker. She had to *do* something . . .

But tonight, her mind would not work. She tried thinking of other things, but her eyes came back again and again to Bob's face. His eyes closed, his mouth resigned, sometimes she shivered as she looked at him. Supposing he never opened his eyes again? Supposing . . .

The doctor came in. A short tubby man with ginger hair and a friendly reassuring smile.

"At least he's no worse," he told Voi. "Actually we're quite pleased with him. You're his girl friend, aren't you?"

Voi nodded. "We . . . we were going to be married," She swallowed. "We still will be . . . " She said, almost as if she was defying Fate.

"I am sure you will . . . " the doctor said and left her.

Now the noisy laughter and voices

from the ward had gone. The patients were settling down, reading, some already asleep.

Voi found herself thinking about her mother and how wonderful Dad had been about Bob. He had driven her down to Esher, or rather to the Beechings' house which was some miles away, had introduced her to Bob's parents, helped draw up the roster, gone with her to the hospital for the first time, prepared her for the unpleasant things that might frighten her, such as the tubes, the hanging bottles and Bob's deathlike look.

Would her mother have been such a help? Voi wondered, and then felt ashamed. It was so easy to blame someone who wasn't there to defend herself. Look at the way she'd been blamed for Bob's silence. It just went to show . . .

Maybe if her mother'd been there, she'd have been just as helpful as Dad, just as loving. Perhaps her mother was one of these unfortunate people who couldn't show love. After all, she must love Dad a lot to be so furiously jealous, mustn't she? Maybe it was partly their own fault, Voi thought. After all, she, Suzy and Robbie were nearly always away and when at home for the hols, they usually had their own friends, their own plans. Maybe they had pushed Mum outside their little circle . . . maybe she wanted them to love her and . . .

On a sudden impulse, Voi tore a couple of sheets out of her pad, and began to write.

She was still writing when Uncle Joe arrived, a tall, neatly-dressed man, with that rarity of today, a monocle.

Voi folded the letter she hadn't finished and stuffed it into her handbag as she stood up. Uncle Joe helped her into her coat and watched with a smile as she tied on her balaclava helmet.

"You're quite something . . . " he said in his slightly snooty voice and smiled. "Bob always had good taste."

Outside the hospital, the cold air seared across her face and then, from a car, a figure emerged. Dad!

"I thought I'd come and fetch you . . . " he said, opening the car door, helping her in. "The dinner was delicious, Voi. Carol said the same. I drove her to Victoria, went and saw some friends, and then thought I'd save you the long walk up to the flat. Tired?"

"A bit," Voi said. She glanced back at the hospital. Although she knew it had to be this way, somehow she always felt she was deserting Bob when she left him.

"I see you had a card from your mother," her father went on, as they slowed up in a traffic block before the lights. "Cape Town looks beautiful."

"Yes. She . . . she seems to be enjoying herself."

"I'm glad. You know, Voi, I hope we haven't made *you* dependent on us. No, I'm sure you're not. That's your poor mother's weakness. She was so dependent on her father, then on me . . . It doesn't do to be too dependent on anyone, Voi. It just doesn't do. It's not fair to yourself, to the one you depend on — or to anyone."

Voi slid along the seat, tucked her hand through his arm. "Don't worry about me, Daddy darling. I'm the independent type," she said, but suddenly she wondered if it was true.

If . . . hastily she corrected herself:

when Bob was well and they were married, it would be awfully difficult not to depend on him, especially if he looked after her and . . . well, surely, if you loved someone? She glanced sideways at her father's grim face. Poor Mum, she thought, closing her eyes, leaning her head against her father's shoulder. Sometimes it seemed as if poor Mum could do nothing right, Voi thought sleepily.

Two days later she found the letter in her handbag, hastily finished it and posted it. But it was only as she dropped the envelope in the letter box and felt it fall from her fingers, that she realised she had sent it surface mail, and not by air! Then she shrugged. At least, it would reach her mother before Christmas. That was the main thing.

Part Three

Part Three

Mary

AS Adrian parked the car in the usual place, Mary looked at The Robin Inn, which still fascinated her though she had been living in it for five weeks. She loved the long white main building with its graciously curved eaves and the masses of creeping plants to give it colour with their lovely purple, crimson and yellow flowers. She loved the wide stoep that went round the building so that you could always sit outside, chasing or retreating from the sunshine as you wished. Indoors it was as colourful, white walls, polished floors with large gaily-patterned rugs. The fascinating dining-room was built out on a great buttress of rock so that when the weather was wild, the sea spray splashed against the windows, while the seagulls were always swooping down, their wide wings outstretched, their curved beaks ready.

Best of all were the rondavels where

they slept, down in a sheltered hollow and less than twenty yards from the sea. Each rondavel had a private bathroom and its own small stoep. She loved swimming in the little cove, running over the hot white sand, knowing she was safe because of the shark nets the hotel had put there to protect the swimmers.

Mary and Adrian strolled across the beautifully velvet-smooth lawns, past two Africans who were weeding, down the wide white steps to the small valley where the rondavels were. Adrian glanced at her.

"Enjoy today?"

He had driven her to Mossel Bay, showing her the beautiful countryside. It had been a long, very hot day.

"Loved every moment of it, Adrian," she said, and turned to smile at him. "I can't thank you enough. First you rescued me when I didn't know where to go and since then you've looked after me so well. It's been absolute paradise . . ."

Putting his hand under her elbow, they went down another flight of steps. "Don't you thank me," he said with a laugh.

"I'm the one to thank you. You saved my sanity. I'm sure if I'd been stuck here on my own, I'd have cracked up. And look at that time when you nursed me. No, Mary, my dear, I'm the one who's grateful."

"I've really helped you?" she said and he heard the wistful note in her voice.

"Really and truly," he said.

They'd reached their rondavels now. Adrian's was next door to hers. Most of the rondavels were occupied, groups of people lying on the white sands with bright red and green umbrellas tilted above them. From the hotel, the Indian waiters came down, immaculately clean in their white uniforms, bearing trays of drinks.

"I feel like a swim . . . " Mary said, glancing at the smooth inviting water in the small cove.

Adrian laughed. "So do I. Let's see who gets changed first . . . "

In her rondavel, Mary quickly undressed and put on her new green bikini. She tucked her hair under a gay, rubber cap and looked in the mirror.

She certainly looked different, she

thought happily. Oh, this was the life. No doubt about it. This gorgeous sunshine, the sudden sea breezes, the quiet graciousness of it all, no need to hurry, to do anything, just to enjoy it all.

As she went outside and saw Adrian standing, she wondered what she would have done without him.

Swimming out into the cove, the water delightfully, refreshingly cool on her hot body, she remembered that first week in Cape Town. How lonely she'd been those first few days. After she'd sent the parcels to England, there'd been nothing for her to do. She had gone on a coach tour but she'd hated being alone. It was the same at the hotel. It was the awful loneliness that she loathed.

Then one day, red roses had arrived, followed by Dirk Paynton. How glad she'd been to see him! How eagerly she'd accepted his invitations and for the next two days they'd driven about the countryside, going up Table Mountain, exclaiming at the fabulous view, then in the evenings they'd dined and danced and she'd enjoyed every moment of it until that last night when he had gone up to her room with her and had walked in, kicking the door shut, taking her in his arms.

Mary rolled over in the cool water and floated, her body moving gently in the swell. She could remember it so plainly. Maybe she'd had too much to drink . . . she didn't know what it was but she had felt herself respond to him, had found her arms round his neck, her mouth waiting for his and then as his hands began to explore, running down her arms, fumbling for her zip, she'd come to her senses. She'd pushed him away.

"Don't do that . . . " she'd said sharply.

He had let go of her. "What the devil d'you mean?" he'd demanded angrily.

She'd stared at him. "I'm sorry, Dirk, but . . . "

"You're sorry . . . " He had stood, legs apart, hands on hips scowling at her. "I should damn well hope so. What's the big idea? I've been pretty patient, you must admit."

"Dirk, I'm married . . . "

"So what? You're game to play around, but so far and no farther, is that it? A tease, that's what you are. The Americans have a better name for it . . . Why've you encouraged me? Practically asked me into your bed . . . "

"I haven't. I thought . . . "

"You thought," he'd said bitterly. "The trouble is you don't know how to think, Mary Herron. You can't think. You're . . . " She could see how angry he was, how he was battling to control himself.

Then he walked to the door. "Thanks for nothing," he said viciously. "Hell, am I sorry for your husband!" he added and slammed the door.

She had stood alone, hands pressed to her face. She had been frightened and shocked — not because of what Dirk had done but because it would have been so easy to forget Garth and morals and . . . For that brief time, she had forgotten everything but her joy at being in Dirk's arms, kissed by him. Love had not entered into it . . . just a physical pleasure.

She'd walked the room that night,

254

thinking, going back down the years, trying to remember. Had she ever felt like that with Garth? No. Yet she loved him. Was it true, then, that you could feel a physical love for someone without really loving them? Not the marrying kind of love?

It was just as she was falling asleep that she remembered Dirk's last words:

'Am I sorry for your husband!'

Mary rolled over in the water and swam leisurely towards the shore, still remembering.

How lonely she'd felt next day. The hours had dragged by and then Victor Courtney had phoned her.

Would she, he wanted to know, care to dine at his house that night? If she was free, he'd send his chauffeur to pick her up.

Her first impulse had been to accept but something had stopped her. Would her acceptance seem like an invitation? she wondered. Would it be seen as encouragement, as a willingness to share his bed? If so, it could only mean another ugly scene. "I'm terribly sorry, Victor," she had said, "but I'm going to stay with some old friends and they're calling for me this afternoon. Some other time perhaps."

"Of course. Just give me a ring when you're available," he'd said but there was an odd note in his voice.

So she'd gone to the receptionist and said she wanted to move to another hotel, preferably out of Cape Town. Could he advise her?

"Most of the hotels are booked out, Madame," he said politely. "You should have tried earlier. Booking for one week only isn't wise at this time of the year, I don't know what to suggest. We're fully booked out and you . . . "

"One week? Oh, yes, of course . . . " She'd remembered that Edith had booked her in at the Waverley for one week only, to give her a chance to look around. And she'd forgotten all about it.

She'd walked out on to the terrace and ordered coffee, watching the couples and groups laughing and talking by the pool, feeling that terrible, horrible loneliness again.

She was suddenly tempted to jump on the next plane and fly back to England.

But even if she did that, she thought, she'd have to go *somewhere*. Mr. Angel had said she and Garth should not meet for six months. It seemed an endless time.

And then Adrian had arrived. Just out of the blue. He seemed delighted to find her in and they'd had a long talk, mostly about Adrian's recurrent attack of enteritis and about two letters he'd got from his children.

"I've got to find somewhere to live," she'd told him finally. "Can you suggest anywhere? I could go up to Jo'burg or Durban but I'd rather stay down here for a while."

His face had brightened. "Come out and see where I am. I think it's super . . . "

So he'd driven her out to The Robin Inn and she'd fallen for it at once.

How helpful Adrian'd been, she thought, as she came out of the water and walked up the steep slope on the hot white sand. It was funny but he said the same. They'd met one another when they both needed someone. Just by chance.

And now they had lived next door to

one another for five wonderful weeks. And never once had he made a pass at her! What a joy it was to be friends with a man who was content to be just a friend. It made everything less complicated and so much more relaxing. Even if, at times, she got a little bored with Adrian's incessant stories of his wonderful children and beautiful wife. Poor Adrian, would his heartache ever heal? she wondered.

Adrian met her. "I say, Mary, mind coming into my hovel? I've got a bad scratch on my back that's hurting. Could you have a look at it? I don't want it to turn septic."

"Of course," she said and they both went into his rondavel.

The green beaded curtains were drawn across the windows filling the small round room with a strange light. The door to his bathroom stood open, his radio was turned on softly.

"Let's have a look . . . " she said and he turned his back, twisting his arm round, to touch a spot with his finger."

She peered closer. "It looks like a bite, Adrian. And it's very inflamed. I've got some ointment and I'll put some plaster on but I think if it isn't better tomorrow, you'd better . . . "

"See a doctor . . . " he said in a resigned voice. "I know. Still, better to do that. Bites and things always go septic on me . . . "

She hurried next door, slipped on her towelling coat, gathered ointment and plaster and hurried back. Funny but Adrian was a bit of a hypochondriac, always worrying about his health. Very different from Garth who loathed being fussed over.

She put on the plaster and he asked her if she'd like a cold drink. Each rondavel had its own small refrigerator.

"Thanks, I would . . . "

They sat on the small stoep, drinking their ice cold drinks. Suddenly Adrian turned with a smile.

"Has it ever struck you what the outside world would think of us?"

She stretched herself happily. "I couldn't care less."

He laughed again. "No, neither could I, but just imagine if your husband walked in. He'd think the worst."

"He would not . . . " Mary was surprised by her own indignation.

Adrian looked amused. "Oh, come off it, Mary. What husband would believe you. I mean, just look at the life we're leading. Who'd believe it was completely platonic?"

"Garth would — if I said so."

"And what's so wonderful about you that you cannot tell a lie? Don't tell me you never lie."

Mary felt her cheeks burning. "Not if I can help it."

"Isn't that splitting hairs. But seriously, Mary, d'you honestly think. . . no, let's say could you honestly expect your husband to believe you?"

"Of course . . . " She paused, her hand flying to her mouth as she looked at him. "Adrian, would you believe your wife under . . . under the same conditions?"

"I'd want to but . . . well, if we're being honest, it seems to me it works two ways . . . "

He leaned forward, offered her a cigarette. Outside the sun was beginning to fall, the sky ablaze with crimson and yellow. Somewhere a dog howled.

"You see, if I was in similar circumstances and told my wife it was purely platonic friendship, I'd expect her to believe me. But if she was the one to tell me, I'm not so sure I could believe her."

"What you mean is — we have different standards? That we expect people to believe us yet we can't believe them?"

"Exactly," Adrian sounded triumphant. "You've put it in a nutshell, Mary. We expect more from others than we are prepared to give ourselves. I know it doesn't make sense but it's human nature."

She stood up. "I think I'll have a bath . . . "

"Okay by me. I'll pick you up in an hour and we'll go up for drinks," Adrian said.

"That'll be lovely."

Mary went back to her rondavel, turned on the bath and soaked in the warm, fragrant water. She wanted to think. She had to think. Things were happening that made her see everything in a different light.

She could have been seduced quite

willingly by Dirk. She'd had to battle with herself . . . didn't that show that she wasn't perfect? Invulnerable. What was the word? Anyhow if she could fall into Dirk's arms . . . hold him close . . . kiss him hungrily . . . then what right had she to judge Garth, even if his relationship with that woman was *not* an innocent one? You'd no right to judge anyone unless you're sure you are perfect yourself, she told herself.

And she'd been so certain, so sure — as she'd said to Adrian — that Garth would believe her, so didn't it follow that Garth had the right to be, and must have been, just as *sure* that she'd believe him?

But she hadn't.

She turned on some more hot water. How would she have reacted, she asked herself, if she'd been in Garth's shoes? If she'd told him the truth — that her friendship with Adrian was absolutely platonic and Garth had called her a liar? Wouldn't she have been furious? Terribly hurt? Unable to stay in the same house with him because he no longer trusted her? she asked herself.

Yet she'd seen *his* leaving her as a sign of guilt!

She got out of the bath and dried herself quickly.

She chose a green evening dress, brushed her hair back from her forehead. Smiled at her reflection and wished Edith was there to see her.

Edith! Mary felt guilty. Oughtn't she to write to Edith and tell her what a wonderful time she was having?

Somehow she hadn't the energy. This heat seemed to exhaust her. Nor was there much time. Adrian couldn't bear to stay too long in one place. He was driven by a strange restlessness so they spent most of their time driving around in his new car that he was so proud of.

A knock on the door. Adrian, of course.

"Come in," she called.

He opened the door.

"Letter for you. Its been forwarded from the Waverley."

"Letter for me? The first!" She took it. Glanced at it. "Oh, it's from Voi. That's my eldest daughter. I'll read it later," she added, putting it on her bedside table.

"Don't you want to read it now?" Adrian sounded surprised.

"I don't think so. She doesn't write often but when she does, she writes reams. It'd take me ages . . . "

"All right. Let's go up . . . " Adrian said.

The truth was, Mary thought, as they walked up the wide stone steps, she was a bit scared about reading what Voi had written. Voi's last words to her had been so cruel, telling her that if she divorced Garth, all the children would go with him because they loved him the best. It had hurt terribly. Nor was it easy to forget what she'd said. Would this letter be a continuation? Was Voi going to scold her, lecture her . . . ?

Over dinner, Adrian suggested they drive into Cape Town next day.

"I want to send the kids some Christmas cards," he said. "I've left it a bit late so I'll have to send them air mail."

"Christmas?" Mary was startled. In this land of sunshine she had forgotten that out here mid-summer was December. "I hadn't realised it . . . "

"It is hard to believe. I'm sending money for presents," Adrian went on. "I ought to have bought them things earlier and posted them. One forgets that at Christmas time with the postal rush, it can take five or six weeks to get a parcel there."

"And Christmas is . . . ?"

"Three weeks away."

"No . . . ? What sort of Christmas do they have out here?"

He laughed. "I guess it depends on your habits. I have heard of people having turkey and plum pudding but with the temperature up in the late nineties, that doesn't sound very inviting. But they have Christmas trees and . . . "

Mary wasn't listening. She was remembering their Christmas tree. It was a real tree with roots and they had been given it three years ago. Each year, they carefully replanted it. Despite its moves, the tree seemed to flourish. Would they be able to use it this year? she wondered. And did Garth know where all the decorations were? Last year, Robbie and Suzy had made a small stable and had painted the small figures, being kept happy indoors during the long wet spell just before Christmas. And would Mrs. White be free to cook the Christmas dinner? And would she remember to push the sixpences and charms into the Christmas pudding? Could Garth cope alone . . . ?

Of course he could, she told herself quickly. Garth could cope with anything. And no one would miss her.

Next day they went round the shops. Everyone was in a Christmas mood. Carols were being sung, everywhere she saw Christmas decorations, everyone was planning for Christmas except . . .

Herself and Adrian.

She grew more and more depressed as the day passed and in the evening Adrian looked at her oddly.

"I think you need a change of atmosphere, Mary. What say we drive up to Johannesburg for a few days, then down to Durban and slowly back here. We can get back in time. They've planned some fun in the hotel for Christmas . . . "

The word was beginning to make her shudder. Anything would be better than waiting here for it to happen.

"It sounds marvellous," she said with a false gaiety. When she went to bed, she saw the letter on the table. She realised with dismay that she'd forgotten all about it. The maid turning down the bedclothes must have found it on the floor.

Mary read the letter through. Then went to stand by the french windows, gazing at the calm little cove with its palm trees moving gently and the wide path of silver across the sea.

Poor darling Voi. Fancy having to cope with such a thing when you're only seventeen, Mary thought. How she must love Bob. Imagine sitting there, hour after hour, watching his face, waiting for him to wake up — or die!

But the words Mary remembered most were those Voi had written at the end of the letter.

"We'll miss you at Christmas. It won't be the same, Mum."

Garth

CAROL was with Garth when the parcel arrived. She'd come round straight from work and had helped Voi get the dinner. Voi was always in a hurry these evenings, eager to get to the hospital.

He and Carol had dined and talked. His plans for never seeing her again had collapsed, somehow. Not every night but quite frequently she dropped in. She and Voi were good friends and Voi seemed to accept the situation for what it still was — a perfectly innocent friendship. At times, he wondered if he was splitting hairs. He knew Carol loved him and he found both comfort and joy in her company. He dreaded the idea of never seeing her again, of being alone . . .

It was a foggy night, bitterly cold, and there was a knock on the door. It puzzled him for there'd been no first buzz from the front door.

He went and opened it. A short, white-haired woman stood there, peering up at him.

"Mr. Herron? The postman brought this after you'd gone to work this morning so I took it in . . . " She held out a parcel.

"Thanks very much, Mrs. er . . . "

She smiled up at him "Miss Kitts. It's no trouble. I assure you. I'm the only person in the house that's in all day so I always take in the parcels."

"It's very good of you."

He closed the door and walked back towards the glowing electric fire, staring down at the parcel in his hands.

"From South Africa . . . " he said slowly, turning the parcel over and over in his hands.

Carol stood up. "Well, open it . . . " she laughed. "You're just like one of my boys. They like to guess what's in a parcel."

It was well packed. At last he'd undone everything. Slowly he took out the claret-red suede jacket.

"Well . . . it's rather nice . . . " he said slowly.

269

Carol laughed.

"The understatement of the year! Try it on."

He took off his coat, put it over a chair back, then put on the suède jacket. It fitted perfectly.

"Very elegant . . . " Carol told him.

Going to the mirror inside the wardrobe he looked at himself. "What Voi would call smooth."

He turned round, looking over his shoulder. "Know something, Carol. I rather like it."

"You'd be an idiot if you didn't," she said. "It's really nice."

He came back to the fire, his hand stroking the soft suède. "I didn't know she knew my size."

Sitting down, he looked through the packing paper.

"No note . . . " he said and was aware of a feeling of disappointment. But then, perhaps that was asking too much? he thought. This, alone, was a gesture.

He was startled when Carol began to collect her things. "Have you got to go at once?"

"Yes. I really must, Garth . . . " she

said and her voice sounded strained.

"Are you all right, Carol? Feeling a bit off?"

She smiled but it wasn't a very good smile. "I am a bit, Garth."

"I'm walking with you to the station . . . "

"No, please, Garth . . . I'll be all right . . . " Carol began.

He wasn't listening. He got his overcoat and thick gloves, and his bowler hat. "Come along . . . " he said and lowered the head of the electric fire.

They walked through the fog-ridden streets in silence. Garth could not get over his amazement at the present from Mary. It was the first time in his knowledge that Mary had bought him anything without first consulting him, worrying about it, asking him if he was sure he would really like it, and finally making him go with her to buy the present.

The warm heat of the Underground swallowed them up. He walked down to the booking office with Carol and smiled at her.

"One thing the train'll be warm. You'll get a taxi at Bexhill, won't you?"

She looked at him. He thought she looked pale.

"Yes, I will. Goodbye, Garth . . . " she said, turned quickly and hurried through, past the ticket inspector.

He walked home slowly, putting his hands in his pockets, shivering a little in the cold gloom. He tried to imagine Mary in Cape Town. How on earth was she managing without anyone to look after her? he wondered.

At home, he had a better look through the brown paper and tissue paper. But there was no letter. He must write and thank Mary for the present. But to what address?

He phoned through to Edith. "Why, Garth, how are you?" Edith said, her voice surprised. "The kids all right? I was at your house this morning and Mrs. White's keeping it looking nice."

"We're all well," Garth said, a little impatiently. "I wondered if you had Mary's address?"

There was a silence that seemed endless.

"You want to write to her?" He thought there was a strange note in her voice.

"Yes, I do. I want to thank her for a present she's just sent me. Edith, I was so surprised. I've never known Mary buy me anything off her own bat, before. This is a suède jacket and it's a perfect fit."

"That sounds good. Maybe Mary's learning to stand on her own feet . . . "

"Edith . . . you blame everything on to me, don't you? Though I know you'll deny it. Is it really my fault that Mary was so dependent on me?"

"Why, Garth, of course not." Edith laughed. "Honestly, I don't blame anyone. Or if I do, it's her parents but then, they didn't mean to harm her, it was just their way of loving. You are coming down for Christmas?"

"Of course. Have you Mary's address?"

"No, Garth, I haven't. I booked her in at the Waverley Hotel but only for a week. I imagine they'd forward letters. Have you had a letter?"

"No, nothing. But she sent the kids a card each when she got to Cape Town."

"She hasn't written to me. Maybe I should be glad for she was beginning to lean on me, too."

"I suppose she's all right . . . " Garth knew a moment of unease.

"We'd soon hear if she wasn't, Garth."

"I suppose so . . . " He put down the receiver almost reluctantly after their conversation slowly drifted to an end.

He went to the mirror again to look at himself. He was acting like a teen-age kid, he told himself, but still felt an absurd satisfaction in seeing how lean the jacket made him look, how well it fitted. He couldn't get over the fact that Mary had bought it on her own, nor that she'd remembered his size.

Next day Voi got a parcel. She looked at the elegant little gold mesh bag.

"It's sweet," she said, tucked it in a drawer and, apparently, forgot it.

Garth was not surprised for Voi had other things to think about. He was only anxious, for each day Voi seemed to grow more pale, more tense. He wished now that he hadn't told her the truth about Bob. Maybe it would have been kinder to let her break her heart over his silence than go through this agony of waiting.

That same day the usual weekly letters came from Suzy and Robbie. Both were thrilled for they'd had presents from 'Mummy'.

"I can't wear mine here but will in the hols. It's super . . . " Robbie printed.

Suzy's letter was longer. Apparently she had a medical box which included a toy stethoscope. "I wish she'd sent me a real one. But maybe it cost too much money."

Garth wrote a letter to Mary. It was surprisingly difficult. He tried a dozen attempts and the final one still read badly. He thanked her for the suede coat. 'It fits perfectly. How clever of you.' Thanked her for the children's presents. Told her about Bob and Voi's long vigil. When he posted it, he felt uneasy. Would Mary find it stilted? Had she made a move and had he rejected it? Yet what could he say? That he had told the truth but that he understood if she found it hard to believe and . . . Well, he'd said all that and she'd refused to listen.

That night after Voi had gone off to the hospital Garth sat by the fire alone. He was puzzled because Carol had not turned up or phoned him. He thought perhaps she was ill. The night when the suède coat had arrived, she'd looked pale and said she felt off-colour.

Yet how could he ring her home address? Supposing her mother answered? Did her mother know Carol was visiting him, that she knew Voi well? he wondered.

The next day he phoned her office. He was told that she had left her job. They sounded rather annoyed about it. When he got home that evening, the letter was waiting for him.

It was short and as stilted as his letter to Mary had been. Briefly Carol wrote that she'd heard from her husband, that they were going to Australia with the children to make a fresh start, and that she hoped his troubles would work out as smoothly as hers were.

He read and reread the letter a dozen times. It was so unlike Carol . . .

Not a word of affection, nor of regret. He remembered she had said that she loved her husband and that if he came back, she'd 'open wide her arms'.

But there was something funny, he felt. Something false about the letter.

He phoned the number in Bexhill.

There was no answer.

That weekend he drove down to Little Common. He told Voi that it was because he wanted to arrange things for Christmas with Mrs. White.

"We've got to make a plan about the holiday, Voi."

Voi was washing up. Now she turned, her hands deep in soap suds, her face worried.

"Dad, can't I stay up here over Christmas?"

"Darling, I'll need your help. And the kids', too. I mean, it's going to be bad enough with your mother away . . . "

She nodded. "Yes, I do see that. I know Bob'd understand. It's just . . . "

He went and put his arm round her. "I know, darling. But if there's any . . . any improvement, the Beechings will let you know and you could come up at once . . . "

Her face brightened. "Yes and Aunt Edith would cope with the kids. They love her."

"I hadn't thought of that."

So he drove down. The trees were stark

and bare against the grey sky. It didn't take long to see Mrs. White and make arrangements, then he walked down the lane to Edith. She was out. So he wrote a note and pushed it under her door and walked back to the house. staring up at the hideousness of it, thinking of the twenty years he'd lived in it.

He drove to Bexhill. Although he was glad for Carol's sake, yet he felt a terrible sense of desolation. She had made such a difference in his life, filled a gap . . .

Filled a gap. The words seemed to ring a bell in his head. Filled a gap.

A gap? Made by what? A gap made by Mary's rejection of him. A rejection begun soon after Robbie's birth, when she devoted herself to the baby and hardly noticed his father, then when Robbie went to school and she joined the various bridge groups, and began to sit on committees, the rejection had widened the gap between them. It was there somewhere that the trouble began — just after Robbie's birth.

He parked the car in a lane leading off Devonshire Road and went into a café. He felt hungry. He ordered and ate, thinking carefully. If only he could pinpoint it. What had happened to wrench them apart, to make Mary turn away from him? If only he could remember. There must be something.

Afterwards, he drove along the front and parked outside the block of flats where Carol lived. He was not sure why he was going there, nor what he'd say when she opened the door. Yet something made him climb the stone steps, push the bell. He had to see her. There was something false about her letter.

Mrs. Walters opened the door. She stared at him and for a moment, he couldn't speak.

"Is Carol all right?"

"Of course she's all right . . . " the old lady said, her voice irritable. "Why shouldn't she be? Personally I think she's mad, going off half-way round the world with the twins, interrupting their schooling, starting all over again in a new country. She's out, finding out about passports and things." She opened the door. "She's got some money saved up but I think she'll be coming back in a few years so it's just a waste. Would you like to come in?"

He hesitated. "I'm afraid I can't wait. It's just I heard she'd left her job and I was worried . . . "

"Left her job! Yes. Walked out on them, losing a week's salary and other perks, into the bargain." The old lady went on, her cheeks flushed. "Crazy, that's what I call it. She had a fine job, we were happy here, the twins love me and . . . " her voice faltered.

He felt sorry for her. She hated Carol's husband and to have him turn up suddenly and whisk Carol off . . .

"Perhaps you could go out and join them later."

"That's what Carol wants me to do. Live with them. I'm not sure I'd like life in Australia. Knowing no one. I think Carol's crazy to go out, a woman on her own with two children . . . "

Garth's mouth was dry. "A woman on her own with two children . . . "

So his hunch had been right! Carol was lying to him. Her husband had not turned up at all. She was merely using him as a weapon — so that she could break things off with Garth, cleanly, neatly, at one blow. No more plans designed to be postponed, no recriminations, no more, 'just one more week'. But why had she so suddenly decided to do this? he wondered as he drove back to London.

Why? She'd given him no hint. There'd been no dramatic farewell.

And then he remembered.

How white she'd grown as he put on the suède jacket. The strained note in her voice. The quick way she'd announced that she must go at once, her distress when he insisted on walking her down to the Underground station.

She'd always told him that he was still in love with Mary. But he'd wondered, he'd never been sure himself. Was it his pleasure at the gift? His obvious delight because Mary had remembered the right size. Had he shown so clearly his relief and pleasure because Mary had made such a gesture?

Brave little Carol. A far finer person than he would ever be.

A clean break. No tearful farewells.

A new life. He only hoped she'd find a man worthy of her.

But he'd miss her, he knew that. He'd miss her very much.

He got home late. Voi had left a casserole in the oven but he didn't feel hungry. He poured himself a stiff drink and went and stood by the window, looking down the road, knowing that he would never see Carol walking along it again.

It hurt. God — how he'd miss her! Yet in a strange way, he was relieved. The decision had been made for him. He felt ashamed. Yet knew it was true. He did love Mary — but he loved Carol, too, in a completely different way. He'd never have had the strength nor the courage to break completely with Carol. She knew that. So she'd done it for him. His eyes smarted unexpectedly. That showed how much she loved him.

A taxi drew up and absurdly, hope soared inside him. Then he saw the driver helping someone out of the car and up the steps. Garth recognised Voi . . .

Had she had an accident . . . ? His thoughts whirled as he raced down the stairs and opened the front door as the taxi-driver had his finger on the bell.

"Dad . . . dad . . . " Voi was all right. She was walking towards him, the man hovering close. "Dad . . . isn't it wonderful? Bob's all right . . . "

And then she was in his arms, clinging to him, sobbing and talking hysterically.

Garth put his hand in his pocket. "What do I owe you?"

The man, burly in a huge overcoat with a cap pulled well down over his eyes, shook his head.

"Nothing. The Doc at the hospital paid."

"Well, thanks just the same for helping my daughter . . . " Garth gave him some money and the man gave a big grin.

"Thank *you*, sir. Good news I take it?"

Garth nodded. "Very good news. Very good indeed . . . " He slammed the front door and helped Voi up the stairs.

"The doctor gave me something . . . he said it wouldn't work until I got home . . . but . . . oh, Daddy, I'm so sleepy . . . " her voice got slower and softer.

"He opened his eyes, Daddy . . . and I rang for the nurse. I talked to him

. . . and . . . then the doctor came and said. 'If you recognise Voi, just open your eyes once and then close them . . . ' and, Daddy, it was wonderful, Bob opened his eyes and looked at me and then closed them. The doctor was thrilled. He said he's sure that everything will be all right . . . we must just be patient . . . Oh, Daddy, I rang his parents and they're on the way but the doctor said it might be hours before Bob wakes up again and not to worry . . . not . . . to . . . "

The Herron Family

Suzy

CHRISTMAS wasn't the same, Suzy thought, as she trailed around after Aunt Edith, helping her decorate the house. Aunt Edith meant well but she did everything differently from the way Mum did things and it didn't look right. Nor had it been the same coming back from school, Suzy thought. The house was so empty. Even if Mum hadn't always heard what was said, she had listened, she had been there, most of the time, and now she wasn't.

They all felt the same. Suzy knew that. For she knew most things. She might only be nine but nowadays, a girl was almost a woman at that age! This Christmas was like a play, everyone acting a part and the actors being what Miss Wolster, who did drama at school, called corny!

"It's no good, Daddy," Suzy said one afternoon as she helped her father dig up the Christmas tree, pot it and take it indoors. "Let's face the truth. It's not the same without Mum. Even the tree doesn't look the same . . . "

"I know, darling," he said, "but . . . "

What a lot of 'buts' the oldies used, Suzy thought miserably. She caught hold of her father's arm. They were alone for once in the big lounge which was festooned with coloured crêpe paper, as they put twinkling silver beads on the tree. "I must talk to you, Daddy."

He squatted on his heels and faced her. The log fire was sparkling and crackling. Suzy could hear Robbie arguing with Voi in the hall as to where the holly should go.

"Mummy always puts it . . . " he was saying.

"Well, Suzy?" her father said.

"Dad, it's no good not facing the truth," she said, trying hard to make him see that this wasn't a joke and that she was deadly serious. "You simply must face facts. Are you and Mummy having a divorce?"

She held her breath, her hands, hidden by a pile of decorations, had their fingers tightly crossed as she stared at him.

He met her gaze with the same seriousness. "I hope not, darling . . . "

She began to relax and then caught her breath again.

"What d'you mean? You *hope* not?"

He sighed, looked round as if wanting to escape, and then stared at her again. "Because I don't know, Suzy. Your mother and I had a quarrel . . . "

"About another woman?"

She saw his skin go red. "Suzy . . . "

"Please, Dad . . . " She pushed off the decorations and caught hold of his hand, holding it to her cheek. "We must talk about it. I'm not a child. I know all about other women and the eternal triangle and all that. She's my mother and you're my father and I must know."

He let out a long breath. "All right, Suzy. There was another woman but she was just a friend. I think you're too young to understand . . . "

"I am not," she said indignantly. "I know all about sex. We talk about it at school. Did you love this other woman?"

"I liked her. We met on the train. We'd sit together and talk. I went to

289

her flat and met her mother and her twin boys . . . "

"Oh! The nice woman Robbie met?"

"Exactly, Suzy. Anyhow, your mother . . . "

"Was jealous?"

He looked surprised. "Yes, I suppose she was. The main thing was she wouldn't believe me when I said we were just friends."

"Were you?"

"Look, Suzy, at your age . . . "

"Look, Daddy, at my age I'm not the infant you were. So you and Mummy quarrelled 'cos she didn't believe you. It seems rather stupid. I mean, Robbie often doesn't believe me and I often don't believe Voi but we don't quarrel and . . . "

"It's different when you're married. Anyhow, Mummy thought it might be a good idea if . . . if we didn't meet for six months and . . . and thought things over."

"About a divorce?"

"I don't know . . . " He was losing his patience, she saw. "Look, Suzy, I just don't know. I can't tell you any more than that. I don't want a divorce. Your mother has no grounds for a divorce, none at all. I just don't know what's going to happen. Is that all you want to know?"

"Yes. Thank you, Daddy . . . " she said and suddenly knew she was going to cry so she jumped up and raced out of the room, upstairs and into the bedroom she still shared with Robbie. She slammed the door shut and flung herself on the bed. Oh, why had parents to be so difficult? Why, oh why, couldn't they think of other people as well as of themselves? How could they bear it if Mummy never came back?

Robbie

"I DON'T like it . . . " Robbie said for the fifth time, his voice firm.

"Well, you do it your way . . . " his father said.

"I don't want to do it my way."

"Well, then, Robbie, what way do you want to do it?"

"I want Mummy to do it her way . . . "

"But Mummy isn't here and . . . "

"Why isn't Mummy here? Is she dead?"

"Good grief, of course not . . . " Robbie saw he'd startled his father. "Most certainly not, Robbie. It's just that Mummy wasn't very well and she went away for this long holiday and . . . "

Robbie stood still and stared at his father. "Suzy says you and Mummy quarrelled."

"Well, suppose we did, Robbie. Lots of people quarrel . . . "

"But they don't go away for six months. Why did Mummy go away and leave us?"

"Robbie, I don't know. I honestly don't know."

"But Daddy, I thought you knew everything . . . "

"Robbie, I only wish I did. Look, come and sit by the fire with me and I'll tell you what I think . . . "

Robbie went and curled up before the fire. He looked up expectantly at his father. "Yes?"

"Well . . . well . . . Robbie, you know how if you do the same thing over and over again, you get bored? Yes, you do know that. Well, and if you're with the same people all the time, soon there isn't anything to talk about?"

"We've always got something to talk about . . . "

His father sighed. "Perhaps one has when one is young but as you grow older . . . Look, what I'm trying to say is that I think Mummy really wasn't well, she needed a complete change, a chance to meet people, to get to know herself . . . "

"I know myself. I don't need to go away . . . "

"Robbie, that's different . . . "

"When's Mummy coming back?"

"When . . . ? Well, in March . . . I think."

"You don't know?" Robbie's voice was a wail. "Then you don't know if she ever will come back . . . "

"No, I don't know . . . " Garth said, standing up and going to the window. "Robbie, I think we're going to have snow. Wouldn't it be nice if we had a lot of snow and could build a snowman?"

"Would it? I don't think anything's nice these days," Robbie said, turning away and walking out of the room.

Voi

DECORATING the house, talking to Aunt Edith, trying to cheer up dismal Suzy and sullen Robbie, Voi felt like screaming. Couldn't anyone see that she shouldn't be here? she thought angrily. Her place was in London, sitting by Bob's side, holding his hand, feeling the slight pressure of his fingers as he tried to move them, talking quietly to him, seeing his eyes flicker, knowing that though he still couldn't move or talk, he could understand. Didn't Dad realise that this was just killing her, tearing her into little bits? This was her mother's job . . . her own place was near Bob.

Why were oldies so stubborn? So proud and stupid? Twenty years of married life and . . . and just because you think your husband has told a lie, you walk out on him. Not only on your husband but — what was infinitely worse — on your children!

295

Was it fair, Voi asked herself angrily, to hurt your children? Did they ask to be born? Did they choose you as parents? Of course they didn't. Children are the parents' responsibilities and it wasn't fair.

It just wasn't fair . . .

Garth

SOMETIMES Garth was glad to have Edith's help. At other times he wanted to tell her to get out — that the only woman he wanted in the house was Mary. What a farce it all was. Putting holly on pictures, decorating the tree, with both Suzy and Robbie fighting him over every small ornament, every strand of silver tinsel, constantly saying:

"Mummy doesn't do it that way . . . "

And the questions! He'd been put through the mill by Suzy and by Robbie. Today, small children thought they had the right . . . well, in a way, they *did* have the right for Mary was their mother.

Even Voi bristled with silent disapproval. She was making a gallant attempt to make Christmas Christmassy for the kids' sake but you could see it was breaking her heart being away from her beloved Bob, who was still just a shell of a man.

Maybe he should have taken the kids

abroad to some sunny place, Garth thought. He could well afford it. Or flown them all out to South Africa and walked in on Mary.

Only he still didn't know where she was. He'd had no answer to his letter of thanks for the suède jacket. Nor had the children heard from her again. Could she be ill . . . or . . . but no, as Edith said, they would have known. He'd been to Bexhill and talked to Mr. Angel who knew nothing. Mary hadn't written to him, either.

"Just be patient, Mr. Herron," the old man said. "I have a strong feeling that the six months will make your wife see everything very differently."

Meanwhile, Garth thought angrily, he was landed with the problem of the children and their questions and their . . . their misery.

They were right, too. Christmas wasn't the same without Mary. Funny, looking back. She was such a vague figure, flickering about, never there when he wanted her and always there when he didn't want her, evasive, uninterested and yet — and yet, he missed her terribly. The house seemed to scream of its emptiness. And that was the way the kids felt. A pretty miserable lot they were and what sort of Christmas were they going to have? he wondered unhappily.

It was two days to Christmas and a horrible day. Not only bitterly cold, not only was there a gale blowing, bending the trees nearly to the ground, playing havoc with the garden, but the sky was grey and packed with dark low clouds. He turned on the lights in the house, had fires lit in every room with a fireplace, the T.V. blaring away and still there was this miserable atmosphere.

Voi, bless her, was being very gay but it screamed of pretence, her face, white and drawn, her ears obviously alert for the phone bell to ring. Suzy pretending to read, hardly answering when they spoke to her. Robbie sitting with his Teddy Bear, an old favourite he had discarded two years before but had now dug out of the attic.

Mrs. White was in the kitchen, singing dolefully. She, too, blamed him, Garth knew that. Oh, she'd never said so in as many words but her whole manner projected an aura of disapproval.

"The poor children," she'd often say without rhyme or reason. "The poor wee kiddies."

Garth stood before the fireplace. He filled his pipe slowly, trying to think of something to do, some idea that might clear the atmosphere, help them to be more cheerful.

And then they heard a car in the driveway and a voice. Garth swung round, pipe in hand, face startled. Voi stood, frozen, by the staircase. Suzy'd dropped her book. Robbie was hugging his Teddy Bear, gazing at the door.

They could see the front door from where they were. It opened slowly.

"Mummy . . . " Robbie dropped his Teddy Bear and was off like a rocket, landing with a bang by her side as she knelt and caught him to her.

Suzy was a close second. "Mummy — is it really you?"

Mary looked up . . .

But was it Mary? Garth stared at her. It was a new, entirely different Mary, he saw. She looked much younger, much more elegant in that Cossack fur hat and fur coat . . .

Something rang a bell in his mind. He remembered the mysterious visitor at the office — who had vanished before he could speak to her. He'd only caught a glimpse of her coat but the receptionist had described her clothes in detail. So that had been Mary . . . Come to make the peace? he wondered. And then had seen him talking to Carol?

He moved forward. "Mary . . . "

She hugged Suzy, kissing her, then stood up, one arm round Robbie. She pulled off her hat and Garth saw that her hair was cut short, naturally curly and was an attractive shade of amber. He saw, also, that she was made-up, subtly, cleverly.

"Garth . . . "

She smiled at him.

"Mum . . . " Voi went forward. "You look marvellous." Voi's voice was respectful. "You look terrific."

Mary turned to her. "Darling . . . thank you. And how's Bob?"

"He's going to be all right . . . he can open and close his eyes to talk and . . . "

"Oh, darling . . . "

Garth saw Mary's face crumple as she caught Voi and held her close, kissing her.

"My poor darling . . . you must have been through hell . . . "

"It wasn't easy, Mummy . . . "

"I'm sure it wasn't . . . "

Garth saw that Mary was trying hard not to cry. Now she glanced at him almost — nervously?

"It's good to see you, Mary . . . " he said awkwardly.

She flashed him a smile. "It's good to be home." She turned to the younger children. "I've a pile of luggage on the doorstep and an awful lot of Christmas presents. Bring them in for me, would you, darlings?"

She looked round. "I see you're ready for Christmas . . . "

"It's not been done right, Mummy . . . " Robbie said, obviously reluctant to leave her side.

"But Mummy can soon put it right," Suzy said. "Come on, Robbie, give me a hand . . . "

They darted out into the cold air and

Mary walked to Garth.

"I see the jacket fits nicely . . . "

"It's super. Did you get my letter?"

She looked up at him. "No. I've been travelling about. I had a wonderful time in Cape Town and then . . . then I went up to Johannesburg and to Durban with a friend and then . . . then it was nearly Christmas and I knew I couldn't stay away any longer. I simply had to come back . . . "

"Why?"

"Because I missed you . . . " Mary paused and added: "all." Garth went to help the children bring in the luggage.

"Get Mrs. White to make some tea, Voi."

Mary laughed. "Don't worry, darling, I will. I must go and thank Mrs. White for looking after you. Oh, it's good to be home . . . " She looked round her. "Good to be with you all." She went out to the kitchen.

He put down the suitcases and saw the way the three children followed their mother to the kitchen.

What does this mean? he wondered. He caught his breath. It was too soon yet to hope but . . .

All through tea, Mary held them engrossed. She talked of the ship. "You'd love it, Voi darling. It's such fun. You do nothing but lie in the sun and dance all night. Then Cape Town is super. We must all go out one holiday, Garth. The children would adore the sands. Oh, and the Game Reserves. I went to one with a friend and I've got some snaps of elephants and lions . . . "

"Real?" Robbie asked. "I've a friend at school whose father is a game warden."

"Is he? I saw baby lions and . . . and monkeys . . . all round you and you drive in your car . . . "

"Were you scared?" Suzy demanded.

Mary laughed. Even her laugh had changed, Garth thought. It was less restrained, more uninhibited, a gayer sound.

"And how! But I realised so long as I stayed in the car I was okay. It was the big elephants that really scared me the most . . . "

"I bet . . . " Robbie murmured, his eyes shining. "It sounds great."

"Oh, it was. And I stayed at a

marvellous hotel. I've got snaps of it, too. I had a rondavel — that's a small round hut with a thatched roof — right on the beach. Every morning when I got up, I'd put on my bikini and race over the sands — gorgeous white sands — to the sea. We swam a lot . . . "

"We?" Garth asked. "You were with friends." Mary looked at him and smiled. "No. With *a* friend. A very dear friend who was trying to recover from a broken heart." Then she turned to the children. "Then we went by car up to Johannesburg. You should see it. Skyscrapers, mine dumps that look like the Pyramids. Traffic and everything moves so fast. It's . . . it's incredible And Durban . . . I've got snaps of rickshaws and their . . . well, drivers I suppose, only they *pull* the rickshaws and they have fantastic bead headdresses. I've got snaps of that . . . "

After tea, she talked to Voi and Garth wasn't surprised when they came to see him.

"Garth, I told Voi she must go back to London at once," Mary said. "I knew you'd agree. Her place is by Bob's side, isn't it." It was not a question, it was a statement. He'd never heard such a decisive note in her voice before.

"I'm ringing the Beechings right away. I'm sure they'll be delighted to have Voi over Christmas. We'll miss her but . . . she should go," Mary continued.

"Yes, I agree." Garth felt slightly stunned. This new Mary was so completely different from the Mary he remembered. Never before would she have expressed an opinion so firmly. In the past it would have been: "Ask your father."

Voi's face was radiant. "Could you drive me to the station, Dad? I won't take long to pack."

"And I'll call the Beechings," Mary said. "Oh, and we must collect our presents for you. Suzy, Robbie, find your presents for Voi . . . and you, too, Garth . . . " She smiled at him. "You've got the Beechings' number?"

"Yes." He gave it to her. "I'll go and get the car . . . "

He came back just as Mary hung up the receiver. She turned and he saw the tears in her eyes as she ran to the stairs.

"Voi . . . Voi . . . good news. Wonderful news, darling."

Voi was at the top of the stairs, almost tumbling down them in her excitement.

"Bob spoke, Voi. He actually spoke. He said: 'Where's Voi?' Oh, Voi, isn't it wonderful . . . "

The two women hugged one another tightly and then Mary moved away, still holding Voi. "The Beechings had just got back from the hospital and were about to ring you. They're absolutely thrilled to hear you're going up tonight. I told them you'd catch the next train and someone will be at Victoria to meet you. Oh, Voi . . . "

Garth sympathised but he saw they were both near tears so he slipped away to his study and took out his present for Voi. He hadn't known what to get her so had played safe and got some very expensive bath crystals.

When he went back to the hall, Voi had vanished and Mary, with Suzy's help, was unpacking one of the suit-cases.

"I've got them all done up and with your names on them . . . " Mary was saying. She took out two parcels, tied with bright ribbon. "These are Voi's."

"You've got something for me, Mummy?" Robbie was looking anxiously.

Mary bent and kissed him. "Of course. And Suzy, and Daddy . . . "

"And Uncle Tom Cobleigh and all . . . " Garth chanted and the children flew at him, laughing and he saw the laughter in Mary's eyes.

As he put on his overcoat, Mary came to his side.

"I want to phone Edith to ask her up for Christmas, Garth. I thought maybe we could ask your friend, Max, too."

Garth grinned. "He'll love that. He's got quite a thing about Edith. Says she's unique or . . . no, I've got it. He said she was something of an enigma."

They both laughed. Shared laughter, he noted with a quick feeling of relief.

"He has? Oh, Garth, what fun. Edith badly needs a man . . . "

He was startled. It was such an un-Mary-like expression. But then everything about her was different. She was a stranger in many ways. An exciting stranger, he thought and laughed at himself. Why, he'd been married to her for twenty years, so how on earth could she be a stranger?

But she was different. Quite different. Much more independent, more sure of herself. The way she'd rung the Beechings unhesitatingly. In the past, she'd have asked him if he thought it a good idea. . . . if they should wait . . . they would have talked about it for more than half an hour before she did anything. She'd always needed reassurance, the certainty that she was doing the right thing. Now she had changed. She seemed to know.

Mary was collecting the presents in a heap. "Not to be opened before Christmas Day, Voi . . . "

Voi hugged her. "Thanks for everything, Mum. I'll phone you . . . "

"I shan't be long. I'll run her down to Cooden," Garth said.

There was a sudden silence. He caught his breath with dismay. But Mary was smiling at him.

"Wouldn't Bexhill be better, darling?" she asked. "It's not nearly so draughty and there's a cold wind blowing."

He drove Voi to the station, they paced the platform till the train arrived. They were lucky, they hadn't long to wait.

"You don't mind me going, Dad?"

He kissed her. "Of course not. It worried me, for I knew how much you wanted to be with Bob, but it was difficult without your mother here."

"Well, now she's back . . . " Voi said happily. "I'm so glad . . . "

So was he, Garth thought, as he drove home through the cold bleak night. But was it for good? Or simply because she didn't want to spoil the children's Christmas? He wished he knew.

When he got back, Suzy and Robbie were curled up on the couch with Mary, the joys of T.V. completely forgotten in the excitement of her snaps and her stories of her holiday.

It was much later that evening before Garth was alone with Mary. He longed for that moment. And dreaded it at the same time.

Mary

MARY was equally nervous. Although she was gay with the children, she was wondering what she should say to Garth and how to go about it.

She tried to remember at what moment she had made up her mind to ignore Mr. Angel's advice and come back. Maybe when she got so homesick seeing all the preparations for Christmas. Perhaps during that long drive through the lovely countryside to Johannesburg — where the Christmas rush was even more evident. It was all so commercial. Perhaps it was the scorching heat, the sun that never ceased to shine, that made it all seem such a false Christmas. As if everyone was pretending it was Christmas in the middle of the summer. Or was it when they drove down to Durban and, once again, Christmas hit her, with the streets decorated and the shops packed with eager shoppers, filling their baskets with food and presents? Or was it the day she realised that while she and Adrian were excellent friends, enjoying one another's company, she was not really *needed* by him? All he needed was a sympathetic ear to listen to his troubles, and she began to see that he was wallowing in self-pity. Was he a masochist, perhaps, delighting in hurting himself by constantly remembering his beloved wife? Or was it, Mary asked herself, the plain simple truth that she wanted to come home?

To come back to them all. To Garth as well as to the children. At what moment had the knowledge come to her that she was still Garth's wife, that she loved him, that she loved the children, that she was utterly miserable?

Adrian had understood. It was exactly how he felt, he said, but she was lucky in knowing that nothing definite had been arranged.

"I'm sure your husband will welcome you with open arms . . . " he'd said, trying, she knew, to hide his own loneliness which was about to start again.

They'd driven back to Cape Town to collect her luggage and Adrian had seen her on a plane to England. She'd decided to come home without warning, hoping to see by their reactions if they really wanted her back or not.

She was not quite sure. The children had seemed delighted, certainly, but Garth?

He had been charming but he hadn't kissed her. He'd been friendly enough, too, but that was all. Was he just putting on an act to make the children happy? she wondered.

At last they were alone. The children asleep, Mrs. White gone home.

Mary put a log on the fire and Garth went to the small bar.

"Like a soft one?"

Mary laughed. "No thanks. I prefer a gin and tonic. I got the habit on the ship."

He looked startled but said nothing. In the past, she'd rarely drunk anything alcoholic except with Edith. Actually, Mary had rather disapproved of women drinking, something that had seemed a big joke to Edith. Doubtless a remnant of parental training and very stupid, Edith had always said.

Now Mary kicked off her shoes, curled up in the deep armchair, and looked at him. The moment had to come eventually and the sooner she got it over the better.

"Were you surprised when I walked in?"

"And how." He grinned. "We'd all been so utterly miserable."

"You had?" She was really surprised. "I thought the children were just being kind to me. You know what a one Suzy is, falling over backwards to avoid hurting people. Did you really miss me?"

He laughed. "I'll say! The children never stopped nagging me because I did everything the wrong way and not 'Mummy's way . . . ' Robbie gave me a lecture so did Suzy . . . "

"A lecture?"

"They seemed to think I should have made certain you were home for Christmas. As they said, it wasn't Christmas without you."

"I'm glad I came but . . . " She took a deep breath. "It needed courage."

314

"Courage?" He was obviously startled. "But why . . . "

She bent down and picked up Robbie's aged Teddy Bear, discarded now.

"Well . . . because . . . because I was afraid I'd left it too late."

"Too late?" Garth was frowning. "I don't get it."

She moistened her dry mouth with her drink, playing for time. But what was the good? she asked herself, it had to be said.

"Yes. I was afraid I'd left it too late to . . . to say how sorry I was for being so stupid."

"Stupid?"

It struck her that now he was echoing her words — whereas in the past, she was the one to do the echoing. Perhaps he realised it at the same moment, for he stood up and came to stand in front of her.

"I was the stupid one," he said. "Expecting you to believe something that no one could ever believe."

She stood up. They were close to one another and yet felt like a thousand miles apart.

"Garth. In South Africa . . . or rather, on the ship, I met a man I grew to like very much. I was sorry for him. He let his wife divorce him for the sake of his children, whom he adores. He's never stopped loving her, either. We were good friends. Mine was the shoulder on which he wept. He looked after me. Garth, have you any idea how lonely one is without one's husband? I used to feel people staring at me, gossiping, perhaps sneering or feeling sorry for me. Adrian took me dancing, swimming, for long drives. He made me laugh, feel needed, he helped me gain a sense of proportion, to see how outdated were some of my ideas. He gave me self-confidence, showed me the world. As you know, I married you practically out of the schoolroom. I'd never had any real fun. Edith used to tell me that and I thought how wrong she was. Now, though, I learned to enjoy life."

She paused. Both were standing very still. The same distance between them.

"Garth, would you believe me when I tell you that it was an innocent relationship? It was. But I wouldn't blame you in the least if you called me a liar. Though it is the truth. I called *you* a liar, but now I know you were telling the truth. I didn't understand how there can be different kinds of loving . . . "

He held her by the arms gently and looked down.

"Mary — I do believe you. But supposing I tell you that I'd lied? That my friendship with Carol Stirn was not a platonic one?"

She swallowed nervously. "I'd forgive you, Garth, but it might take a little time. I do realise, now, that . . . well, that things can happen."

"Did they happen to you?" he asked, his face suddenly stern.

She shook her head. "No, but they nearly did. I'd been drinking and . . . I was, well, I was surprised and rather shocked at myself . . . "

"And the man?"

"He was furious with me. Called me a . . . a tease . . . said he was sorry for you . . . "

Her voice was suddenly uneven as she

wondered where this conversation was taking them.

"Garth, I am sorry. I know it was my fault. Right from the beginning. Is it too late . . . too late for us to start again."

He moved swiftly and pulled her into his arms. "Too late! Don't be daft, darling. It could never be too late for I could never stop loving you. That's the truth . . . " He kissed her. She put her arms round his neck, pulling his head down to kiss him.

"Oh, Garth . . . I'm afraid I'm going to cry . . . " she whispered.

"You'd better not or I'll beat you . . . " he said happily, swooping her up in his arms, dropping her on the couch, kneeling down by her side, and kissing her again.

"Oh, what fools we've been, Mary love. What utter fools . . . "

She kissed the corners of his mouth. "Darling, I really love you . . . " she said.

"Thank God, but d'you have to sound so surprised . . . ?"

She held him close. "Yes — for sometimes I wondered."

"So did I . . . " he said truthfully.

He sat back on his heels, holding her hand tightly.

"You are back for good?"

"If you really want me . . . "

"Of all the stupid questions . . . "

He leant forward and kissed her again. It was quite some time before she pushed him away gently.

"Garth, I've been thinking. Wouldn't it be fun if we sold the house and the furniture? After all, we never chose any of it ourselves. It'd be like getting married all over again, wouldn't it? I think it would be nice to live nearer London, then I can go up more often and you wouldn't have to commute so far and we'd be nearer the children and . . . and I think Voi is going to need a lot of moral support in the near future, for Bob isn't going to recover overnight and . . . " she stopped, breathless, a condition which was not improved by the fervour with which Garth began to kiss her.

When she could, she broke away. "You're sure you'd like to do that?"

"Quite." A kiss.

319

"Quite." Another kiss.

"Sure."

"Good. There's just one other thing, Garth. I think I was bored here. I don't really like bridge or committees but I was bored and Edith suggested it and . . . what I'm trying to say is . . . well, Garth . . . don't you . . . don't you think it's time we had another baby."

He held her so tightly she could hardly breathe. Then he let her go and smiled at her.

"That's the best idea I've heard for years. The sooner we . . . "

But she stopped him, her face suddenly grave.

"Garth — help me. Be patient, darling. I know I was a lousy wife . . . " She put her hand on his mouth. "No, let me finish, darling. I do love you so and I will try to make you happy . . . "

He brushed her hand away.

"You say the most stupid things, Mary. I'm the happiest man in the world already."

He ceased speaking and began to kiss her. As her arms tightened round his neck, she made no attempt to stop him. After all, all that had to be said had been said.

THE END

Other titles in the
Ulverscroft Large Print Series:

TO FIGHT THE WILD
Rod Ansell and Rachel Percy

Lost in uncharted Australian bush, Rod Ansell survived by hunting and trapping wild animals, improvising shelter and using all the bushman's skills he knew.

COROMANDEL
Pat Barr

India in the 1830s is a hot, uncomfortable place, where the East India Company still rules. Amelia and her new husband find themselves caught up in the animosities which seethe between the old order and the new.

THE SMALL PARTY
Lillian Beckwith

A frightening journey to safety begins for Ruth and her small party as their island is caught up in the dangers of armed insurrection.

THE WILDERNESS WALK
Sheila Bishop

Stifling unpleasant memories of a misbegotten romance in Cleave with Lord Francis Aubrey, Lavinia goes on holiday there with her sister. The two women are thrust into a romantic intrigue involving none other than Lord Francis.

THE RELUCTANT GUEST
Rosalind Brett

Ann Calvert went to spend a month on a South African farm with Theo Borland and his sister. They both proved to be different from her first idea of them, and there was Storr Peterson — the most disturbing man she had ever met.

ONE ENCHANTED SUMMER
Anne Tedlock Brooks

A tale of mystery and romance and a girl who found both during one enchanted summer.

CLOUD OVER MALVERTON
Nancy Buckingham

Dulcie soon realises that something is seriously wrong at Malverton, and when violence strikes she is horrified to find herself under suspicion of murder.

AFTER THOUGHTS
Max Bygraves

The Cockney entertainer tells stories of his East End childhood, of his RAF days, and his post-war showbusiness successes and friendships with fellow comedians.

MOONLIGHT
AND MARCH ROSES
D. Y. Cameron

Lynn's search to trace a missing girl takes her to Spain, where she meets Clive Hendon. While untangling the situation, she untangles her emotions and decides on her own future.

NURSE ALICE IN LOVE
Theresa Charles

Accepting the post of nurse to little Fernie Sherrod, Alice Everton could not guess at the romance, suspense and danger which lay ahead at the Sherrod's isolated estate.

POIROT INVESTIGATES
Agatha Christie

Two things bind these eleven stories together — the brilliance and uncanny skill of the diminutive Belgian detective, and the stupidity of his Watson-like partner, Captain Hastings.

LET LOOSE THE TIGERS
Josephine Cox

Queenie promised to find the long-lost son of the frail, elderly murderess, Hannah Jason. But her enquiries threatened to unlock the cage where crucial secrets had long been held captive.

THE TWILIGHT MAN
Frank Gruber

Jim Rand lives alone in the California desert awaiting death. Into his hermit existence comes a teenage girl who blows both his past and his brief future wide open.

DOG IN THE DARK
Gerald Hammond

Jim Cunningham breeds and trains gun dogs, and his antagonism towards the devotees of show spaniels earns him many enemies. So when one of them is found murdered, the police are on his doorstep within hours.

THE RED KNIGHT
Geoffrey Moxon

When he finds himself a pawn on the chessboard of international espionage with his family in constant danger, Guy Trent becomes embroiled in moves and countermoves which may mean life or death for Western scientists.

TIGER TIGER
Frank Ryan

A young man involved in drugs is found murdered. This is the first event which will draw Detective Inspector Sandy Woodings into a whirlpool of murder and deceit.

CAROLINE MINUSCULE
Andrew Taylor

Caroline Minuscule, a medieval script, is the first clue to the whereabouts of a cache of diamonds. The search becomes a deadly kind of fairy story in which several murders have an other-worldly quality.

LONG CHAIN OF DEATH
Sarah Wolf

During the Second World War four American teenagers from the same town join the Army together. Forty-two years later, the son of one of the soldiers realises that someone is systematically wiping out the families of the four men.

THE LISTERDALE MYSTERY
Agatha Christie

Twelve short stories ranging from the light-hearted to the macabre, diverse mysteries ingeniously and plausibly contrived and convincingly unravelled.

TO BE LOVED
Lynne Collins

Andrew married the woman he had always loved despite the knowledge that Sarah married him for reasons of her own. So much heartache could have been avoided if only he had known how vital it was to be loved.

ACCUSED NURSE
Jane Converse

Paula found herself accused of a crime which could cost her her job, her nurse's reputation, and even the man she loved, unless the truth came to light.

BUTTERFLY MONTANE
Dorothy Cork

Parma had come to New Guinea to marry Alec Rivers, but she found him completely disinterested and that overbearing Pierce Adams getting entirely the wrong idea about her.

HONOURABLE FRIENDS
Janet Daley

Priscilla Burford is happily married when she meets Junior Environment Minister Alistair Thurston. Inevitably, sexual obsession and political necessity collide.

WANDERING MINSTRELS
Mary Delorme

Stella Wade's career as a concert pianist might have been ruined by the rudeness of a famous conductor, so it seemed to her agent and benefactor. Even Sir Nicholas fails to see the possibilities when John Tallis falls deeply in love with Stella.

MORNING IS BREAKING
Lesley Denny

The growing frenzy of war catapults Diane Clements into a clandestine marriage and separation with a German refugee.

LAST BUS TO WOODSTOCK
Colin Dexter

A girl's body is discovered huddled in the courtyard of a Woodstock pub, and Detective Chief Inspector Morse and Sergeant Lewis are hunting a rapist and a murderer.

THE STUBBORN TIDE
Anne Durham

Everyone advised Carol not to grieve so excessively over her cousin's death. She might have followed their advice if the man she loved thought that way about her, but another girl came first in his affections.